**Praise for** *Elephant and Rabbit and Skib: More discourses from the Magical Forest*

*"Alice in Wonderland meets Beckett!"*

- Roger Hendricks Simon
*The Simon Studio, NYC*

*Visit* **The Magical Forest Gallery** website to hear Roger read seven stories from where it all began:

**Elephant and Rabbit As Told By Skib Bricluster**

**themagicalforestgallery.com**

# T. A. Young

*more discourses from The Magical Forest*

# Elephant and Rabbit

## and Skiß

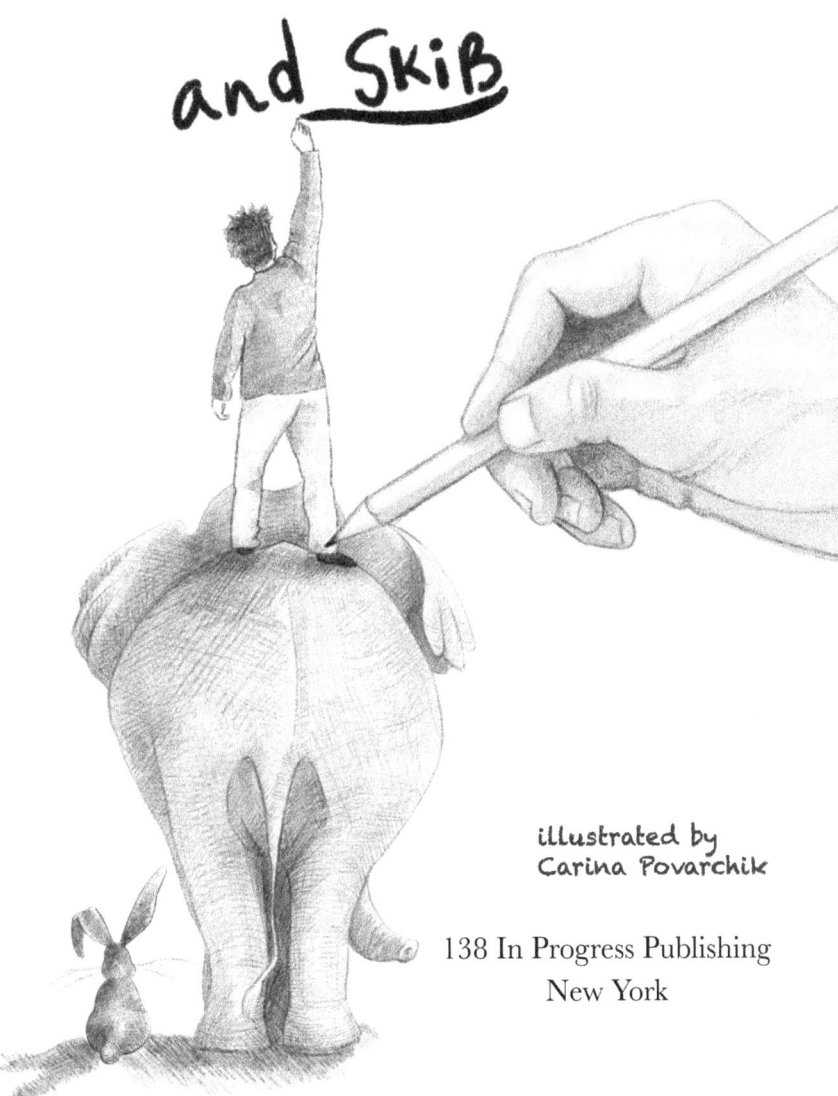

illustrated by
Carina Povarchik

138 In Progress Publishing
New York

© 2023 T.A. Young

All rights reserved, including the right of reproduction in whole or in part in any form.
Published by 138 In Progress Publishing,
Dover Plains, New York.

www.138inprogresspublishing.com
mariangrudko@138inprogresspublishing.com

First Edition: January 2023
Printed in the United States of America

ISBN: 979-8-218-05928-6 (paperback)

Young, T.A.
Elephant and Rabbit and Skib

This book is a work of fiction. Any references to historical events, real people or real locales are used fictitiously.

Edited by Marian Grudko

*Cover design, cover art and interior illustrations by*
*Carina Povarchik*
*by.catru@gmail.com*

*Book formatted by Elliot Toman*
*www.asubtleweb.com*

*This book is for Andria, Victoria, Taylor,
and good ol' Davy:
my magical forest.*

*And for Marian Grudko, co-architect and docent.*

# CONTENTS

## I. More Stories from the Magical Forest — 13

1. Love — 15
2. Rabbit and Elephant Meet a Ladybug — 19
3. Elephant, Rabbit and Shadow as recorded by Skib Bricluster — 23
4. Elephant, Rabbit and Tulip — 28
5. Li-Po and Elephant and Rabbit — 33
6. Elephant and Rabbit and Skib Redux — 37
7. Nullibiety — 44

## A few words from the...author? — 56

A few words from the...author?
...and a word from Rabbit

## II. To The Diner - And Beyond — 61

1. The Night Manager, Misunderstood — 63
2. Frames — 67
3. Frames versus Palimpsests — 70
4. And Another Thing: A Dialogue — 72
5. Between Rounds (The Fighting Kind, Not the Good Kind) — 76
6. The Rig and the Gig — 81
7. A Note — 83

| | |
|---|---|
| 8. Two Months Later ( And The Concrete Temporality Should Be A Clue) | 84 |
| 9. The Quandary Qontinued | 88 |
| 10. An Abrupt Change of Venue | 95 |
| 11. The Ironically Named "Inviting Beach" | 100 |

## III. Presume Not the Carrots       104

| | |
|---|---|
| 1. Presume Not the Carrots (a.k.a The Carrot Episode) | 107 |
| 2. A Visit To A House of Worship (It's Called Balance) | 115 |
| 3. An Example of Why Trees Shouldn't Be Asked Questions | 121 |
| 4. And We Come Full Circle | 126 |
| 5. And We're Back | 129 |

## IV.  Why Not?       131

| | |
|---|---|
| 1. Acting: A Play | 133 |
| 2. A Little Etymology | 142 |
| 3. Man and Nature | 144 |
| 4. Enough Rhetoric: Let's Get Deep! | 146 |
| 5. Snakes | 148 |
| 6. Music is Awesome | 151 |
| 7. Finishing the Tour Thing | 156 |
| 8. A Prelude to Something | 158 |
| 9. We Don't Know: We Haven't Written This Yet | 160 |

## V. The Other Side of the Rabbit Hole — 163

Elephant and Rabbit and Didi and Gogo — 165

## VI. The Return from the Rabbit Hole — 173

1. The Return from the Rabbit Hole, With Relief and Gratitude to Those Responsible — 173
2. A Note — 176
3. One for the Road — 179
4. And One More: Layers — 184

## The Road to When: *"...Et Divisit Lucem A Tenebris"* — 187

1. The Road *Of* When: a lexington-avenue-6-subway-line diatribe by Charley Manheim — 189
2. Thus Spoke Charley — 193
3. The Nymph's Reply — 197

## Epilogue — 201
Epilogue: Meaning the Beginning — 203
Postlude — 207

Closing poem and illustration — 214

Rabbit looked around. "Should we get started? We have a lot to cover."
Elephant was thrilled: he loved beginnings so much more than endings.

And so they began.

# I

*More stories from The Magical Forest*

# 1

# Love

Of all the sights Elephant and Rabbit had ever seen coming down one path or the other, this one ranked pretty darn high. It was a woman of about eighty dressed in matching floral pants and jacket and flats, pulling a mannequin that was somehow attached to a small carpeted dolly.

As she approached, the mannequin became remarkably life-like, and by the time she reached our two heroes, the mannequin was no longer a mannequin but either a terrific waxed figure or - heaven forfend - a human glued to a dolly.

She stopped. "Woosh, I'm pooped."

Rabbit offered her a seat on a tree trunk in the shade. 'Elephant, see if we can find some water for the lady." Elephant dashed off.

Rabbit looked at the figure, then asked a question clearly beneath him: "Is there a story behind this?" He gestured towards the frozen figure.

"Oh, this is my husband, Phil. We're married sixty years now. Look at that face! How could I bury the man of my life? How could I live without him? So, I had him stuffed. Didn't they do a terrific job? He looks happier now. Is this a dream?"

"You show up here with a stuffed husband on a dolly and you're asking me if this is a dream? I should be asking that question."

Parenthetically, it's interesting to note that the matter of a talking Rabbit never came up, almost never comes up in these situations. We're going to have to consider this, someday. Talking animals are usually a tip-off to something different. We can be wonderfully receptive or accommodating or unfazed at times. At others, we freak out over the silliest, most quotidian problems. Oh, no! I left my lunch in the fridge! Dear lord! My birthday's in two weeks! What the hell! I'm almost out of paper towels! Come on: we're better than this.

"I don't know where I am. I was taking Phil to the beach for a little air; Murray and Zel are there with that picnic basket and that dog that never shuts up. I put the sunscreen on our faces and we're almost there, then all of a sudden, just like that, we're here in the woods! Fort Lauderdale, this isn't. So, I'm asking. I didn't have a breakdown or god forbid a stroke or something, did I? God forbid. If I wake up in a hospital, just kill me. But have me stuffed, so I can be with Phil. Call my sister. I'll write down her number...."

"Don't panic. You aren't in a hospital. You're fine. You just went down a different street, but you're close to home."

Rabbit went over to her just as Elephant reappeared with a bowl of water and put it in her hands. She drank and sighed. "I feel much better. I like the air here. Cooler. Not so much with the humidity. Back home, you sweat from the heat."

"So, Mrs----------------------. Just take it easy and we'll get you home."

"No rush, no rush. Phil looks happy here. We're comfortable. A chair would be nice. I was going to put Phil in a chair, instead of standing, but all that sitting isn't good for you. The circulation and all that. But I was worried about him falling over. Anyway, the taxidermist – this fellow, Ludd Whachadoin – do you know him by any chance? – he did our dog, Yutzy – a complete moron – the dog, not Ludd – so, Ludd said he should stand. For the height factor. So we did."

Rabbit was looking at his wrist, imagining a watch was there. He said, "Yeah. No, we don't have any chairs close by. Down the lane a bit, though...."

Elephant asked, "Can we summon a chair?"

Rabbit looked at him. "Summon a chair? What the heck does that mean? Summon a chair!" (Where's an interrobang when you need one?)

"Well, I thought because this is the magical forest we could…you know…"

The woman said, "This is fine. This is fine." Resting her palms on the tree trunk, she closed her eyes to feel the air around her. She liked it, Phil liked it – allow us to attribute this to him: all was right with the world.

She stood up and looked at her husband, picked up his leash and turned to say goodbye to her hosts. Her foot slipped out of her shoe; when she looked down, her toes were covered in sand. The ocean thought that was a good one.

# 2

# Rabbit and Elephant Meet a Ladybug

**(what *really* happened when Claudine first got to Paris)**

R abbit and Elephant were, you know, doing nothing, when a ladybug approached them.

She looked around and knew that she wasn't in Paris, which was perfect because she wanted to be in the magical forest. She was on a mission.

"My name is Claudine, and I have come to understand that this is where I can get some help for a problem I'm having."

Rabbit said, "Claudine, it's a pleasure. I'm Rabbit. This little fella behind me is Elephant.

I assure you," said Rabbit, "you've come to the

right place. We have all the answers. Literally, every single one of 'em. We're up to our necks in answers. We just have trouble connecting them to the right questions. Not easy, I can tell you."

"Yes," said Claudine, holding on to her hope which was only slightly frayed by Rabbit's comment. "You see, I'm a ladybug."

"Got it. Not a pterodactyl."

"Yes, but I feel….no, I might be destined to be human. A beautiful Parisian woman strolling down the boulevard in my Dior dress and…"

"Hold on. Human?"

"I feel it. I know it. I'm much, much more than a ladybug. A bug on a leaf! Oh, dear, no."

"Well, you've successfully offended about a bajillion of your fellow bugs, but go on."

"Oh, there's nothing wrong with being a bug if you're meant to be a bug, but that may not be my destiny."

"You must be loaded with friends." Then Rabbit turned and asked Elephant, "Elephant, what are you?"

"I'm a Whooshponder."

"Were you meant to be a bird?"

"I don't know what I was meant to be. I only know what I am."

"Would you like to be a bird?"

"Sometimes. Can that happen?"

"Would you like to be a human?"

"Ick!"

"Claudine wants to be human."

"But she's so pretty."

"Yep. She makes a terrific ladybug."

"What is she going to do?"

"Ask her."

"What are you going to do?"

Claudine fluttered. "I...."

Rabbit said, "Uh-huh."

"I....I thought this was the magical forest. I.....Where is the magic?" Claudine looked in all directions as if it were around somewhere, which is funny because it sure was.

"Classic misunderstanding," said Rabbit. "Creatures – especially humans - think that magic isn't logical. That it is unreasonable...I mean in both senses. Magic is perfectly reasonable, but some creatures simply aren't."

Claudine was baffled, but because she was strong, she only sighed.

Rabbit did his usual terrible job at consolation. "Look, there is magic in Paris, from what I hear. Go back and give it a shot. Maybe if enough humans see you as human, you'll become one. Big whoop, as far as I'm concerned, but like they say, *'chacun à son goût.'*

"Come back anytime. We're right next door, open 24/7, like a diner, but without the waffles. Or in your case, croissants."

Claudine graciously expressed her thanks. "I

hope we meet again," she said.

"Anytime," said Rabbit. And off she flew.

Elephant said, "She was nice. And so pretty. I guess they don't have mirrors in Paris, so she never got to see herself."

"Trust me, Paris is loaded with mirrors. They just don't work the way they're supposed to."

"That's dumb. How do you make a mirror that doesn't work?"

"That's easy: just have a human make it. They do very few things correctly. Sometimes I wonder if it's intentional. But they certainly got waffles down."

# 3

# Elephant, Rabbit and Shadow as recorded by Skib Bricluster

The sun shone, but it was dark. To quote Bruce Springsteen, "Anyway, that's just a lie": The darkness was not in the sky or below the sky, but on the ground and only the ground, as if the light stopped short one Planck Length above the ground. Or maybe two.

Elephant looked up at the blue, blue sky and did not do what elephants are trained to not do, which is look directly at that piercing yellow disk that is the sun. (The moon doesn't pierce, so there should be no confusion here.)

So: the sun shone down and, typically, shade was created by the trees and leaves and tall rocks and rich foliage, rich because in its entire existence it had never been stood on, trampled, mowed, cut, hewn, or made familiar with clippers, shears, or blades of any kind. Unspoiled, untouched, it grew the way it was meant to grow. If we knew what the heck a metaphor was, we'd say this could be one of them; maybe humans should be allowed to grow this way, untrampled, unmown, uncut, unhewn, unshaped, and so on. You know: free.

But the sun wasn't making it all the way to the ground, unimpeded, though there was nothing to cause the impediment.

Elephant said, "Something isn't right, here."
Rabbit asked, "Do you mean not right or just not normal?"
Elephant: "Yes, strange, I mean."
Rabbit said, "Strange it is. Look around you. What do you see?"
Elephant did a couple of slow spins. He knew better than to miss anything when he was having these lesson-conversations with Rabbit. "Just a tiny bit of grass and some, I guess, ground."
Rabbit asked, "Do you see any trees?"
Elephant pointed with his trunk. "Way over there a ways. On the other side of the rock, there."
"Good. Now what do you see on the ground?"
Elephant looked down, then up, then down, then

up. He looked all over. He lowered his head to study what they were standing on. What he saw were shadows. Of trees and flowers and all that cool flora that filled the forest. Yet there were no trees or anything to make those shadows.

"The shadows. These shadows…. What…. Where…. are they coming from? What is making them? They're real! I can see the branches and everything! Are the trees invisible? I mean, are they there, but we can't see them? Just their shadows?" Boy, was he knocked out.

Rabbit: "Okay. First of all, calm down. Yes, this is pretty cool, but I don't want you getting upset or getting the wrong idea." He paused because he was about to give him the wrong idea, but it was the only one he had. "This is very tough. I don't get it either. But the fact is, the trees and stuff are there, but they are not invisible, but you can't see them. The only way we know they're there is because of their shadows."

Elephant: "The wrong idea? But…" He stopped because he was looking down and saw what was not there among those perfect shadows: his own. "My….But…Where's *my* shadow? Where's *your* shadow? All these…."

Rabbit told him again to calm down. "I can explain. I really can." He really couldn't.

"But aren't we here? How can what *isn't* here have a shadow, and what *is* here, *not* have a shadow?

I mean, you *say* they're here, but…"

(We pause here to commiserate with Skib because he was working hard to get the intensity of Elephant's bafflement down on paper. All those unfinished sentences. All those italics, which in Skib's notebook were underlined words.)

Rabbit spoke sympathetically, yet with the hint of pedantry that we've all come to know and accept, if not embrace. "I'm not saying they're here; you can see they're here." He pointed down. 'We are in a different part of the forest. A different place. You know it's funny about this place." (He paused to muse, then resumed.) "It's funny. Different, yet the same. Same forest, different forest. You really have to think hard when you say, 'This is someplace else.' You have a lot of explaining to do. (Another pause to muse.) But here we are. This is the place we call the Shadow Forest. The trees aren't invisible. You're looking at them. They are made of shadows, bark and branches, leaves and nests, heart and soul. We are just visitors. Our shadows are not part of this place."

Elephant sat, then lay down. "I'm exhausted. This is too much."

Rabbit smiled and then said, not without a tinge of urgency, "Take a breath or two. I know this is a kick in the tail. But it's good to know. Good to know.

But we have to go now. The Shadow Forest could possibly misunderstand your lying down. It may think you're knocking on the door. Like you want in. Not now, old friend. Not yet."

Elephant understood maybe 73% of this, but that was enough for him to find his legs. They walked aways, Elephant looking down so intently, he missed the part where there were real trees — no, not real trees — but solid trees casting shadows. Rabbit saw this and said, "Hey, look!" Elephant raised his head and literally went straight to the closest tree — it was Sylvan The Oak — and wrapped his trunk around his trunk (hey, it happens) and rested his head on Sylvan's trunk. He was almost crying. Even Rabbit was touched. Sometimes we really need to be reminded.

# 4

# Elephant, Rabbit and Tulip

It was early spring that morning.

This requires some kind of context, some kind of explanation, or you'll think we have a syntax problem.

So: someone had sped up the seasons that day, and that person was Lachesis. Yep, one and the same. She was always playing around with Time in the magical forest; sometimes speeding it up, sometimes slowing it down, and very often bringing it to a complete stop. Elephant and Rabbit would be sitting at their favorite spot overlooking the lake and they would see that the surface was as flat and still as glass, and a leaf or bit of pollen stuck in mid-air. And the clouds, motionless. Sometimes birds would be free to fly through or around them; other times, they would be little V's drawn on a blue canvas. With sweeping inclusiveness, sometimes with awful exclusiveness, she toyed with individual creatures minding their own business who were suddenly very much not what he or she or it was before she tinkered with them.

Because it was decided—ha! Decided! How about pure whimsy?—to be early spring that morning, the vernal vanguard jumped into position: the tulips and daffodils – the early risers –did their efflorescent thing, which is like reveille for the rest of the magical forest.

Tulip the Fairy awoke and the forest was awash with faunal pandiculations.

Blessed and cursed as she was, she said to herself, "But if we're here, winter must be coming very soon!"

Tulip had lots of friends, but chose to stand apart, by herself. Here was some tall grass, a tree stump that contained the memories of a great maple that had offered wonderful shade, and a rock that was often the lounging area of Jabari the Chameleon. But she was the only Tulip.

That tree stump – like everything in the magical forest if you look closely enough – held more than memories; in its center was a crack that ran almost its diameter and from deep within grew grass and an odd flower or two and, in time (whatever the heck that was) a glorious medley of fauna will spring in generous and appreciative glory, the trunk hidden and immersed in itself and its new self, and bees will hover and ants will meander and all that other evidence that it had never died, but transfigured into another splendid form. Being close to this, sharing the same soil, made Tulip feel happily connected, which belied – at least a bit – her dread of transience.

She looked across the narrow path at her friends. They smiled and waved in unison abetted by the gentle back-and-forth breeze. Funny, she thought, how the breadth of a narrow path can be both so small and so great, how sometimes distance can be both so close and so far.

Elephant remembered her from last spring. Her sturdy wings and petals, the tides of yellow and white, and one strong, unchallenged line of purple. That was her voice; she called him over, never having seen a Whooshponder before.

"Who are you?" he asked.

"I'm Tulip the Fairy. Who are you?"

"I'm Elephant. Rabbit's friend." He pointed to him with his trunk.

"Ah, Rabbit! He is well known in the forest. He is good. A good soul. A good friend to have - I can tell."

"Are there bad creatures?" asked Elephant. "I've

never seen one."

"The good tend to see the good. Evil is hard to see with a kind heart. Especially the darkest kind." She smiled. "You are in a good place." She paused, then said, "Because you belong here."

Rabbit listened. He knew the power, the vision of Tulip the Fairy. He closed his eyes, taking in her words. He wished that 'gooder' was a word because she was; and she was from a place even 'gooder' than the forest. And though she disliked winter, she did not fear it, only the interruption in her flowering, the requisite folding and fading and sinking back, away from the sun that bothered her. "Better" is good, but "gooder" is better because it has "good" right there.

Tulip appeared to shudder. It may have been the wind, but it was more likely the thought of winter. She said, "The funny thing is, I like snow. I see it above. And above. It's beautiful, but I don't like the wait. I spend a great deal of time waiting, and so little above, feeling the sun, the rain, the winds, the creatures who visit and sometimes rest on my wings and petals, my friends."

"But don't you have time? Until then?"

Tulip smiled again: "That's something I'm not able to see. None of us are allowed to know the greatest secret of all: How much time. Look, now: only this morning, it was spring. Now, we feel the heat of summer and already – Look above! – the leaves begin to wilt and grow sere looking for a place to fall. By night, it will be winter. And the next time, will the gift of Time, the seasons, be longer or shorter?"

Elephant was entranced by her words and her aura. "How do you know so much? So well?"

"Time," she said, and laughed.

*This story is dedicated to Tulip the Fairy, who lives in Brisbane, Queensland, Australia.*

# 5

# Li-Po and Elephant and Rabbit

It was late in the evening in Autumn in the magical forest; the sun had finished her run for the day and only the most begrudging residual rays followed behind her as she headed for the bar. It was Autumn because somebody said so. *Et facta est.*

And sitting on a rock, back to back were Elephant and Li-Po, the legend. Li-Po recited a poem he had just composed that, when it was set on paper, would be entitled "Questions Answered." The poem went like this:

*You ask why I live
Alone in the mountain forest,
And I smile and am silent*

*Until even my soul grows quiet.*
*The peach trees blossom.*
*The water continues to flow.*
*I live in the other world,*
*One that lies beyond the human.*

He spoke the words as if he were speaking to someone, explaining something urgent yet commonplace, sublime yet unremarkable; stunning yet indistinct. He was speaking as if what was visible and palpable to him was visible and palpable to everyone. He reached into the pond with his index finger and shifted the moon a few inches to the right. The moon overhead responded accordingly. None of this is weird or outrageous or mystifying. It is merely true.

What made this little episode marvelous was that Elephant was crying. Not loudly, not heaving or sobbing or sighing, but with elephantine immobility: down the tears ran. He gently used his ears to wave away the wetness.

Rabbit, sitting at the base of the rock – a position determined by the fact that an Elephant and a samurai poet took up all the space there was on the rock, leaving Rabbit to lounge three feet, six inches below, was touched by a tear. He looked up, which tells you that he was physically touched and not –yet – emotionally touched by the aforementioned tear.

Rabbit was going to ask what the tears were

about, but being quite the rabbit, he could discriminate the type of tear with the accuracy of a psycho-bio-chemical-forensic engineer: sadness was not in this tear; this was the kind of tear generated from witnessing overwhelming beauty. The presence of Li-Po made this determination inarguable. Rabbit had had the same response to the poet's words years ago:

> *I slip into a sea of leaves*
> *And waves made of charitable air*
> *I need not reach to touch*
> *Your silence sings my peace*
> *Your song whelms this*
> *Ship that venerates the stars*
> *As they venerate the soul*
> *At the helm, broad-chested,*
> *Unsurpassingly brave, but*
> *Not brazen,*
> *For the sea of leaves gives*
> *Light and takes it away,*
> *Whispers secrets to make men,*
> *To test men, to give them succor.*
> *The wise man does not make the sea*
> *Of leaves a crucible, for therein lies*
> *Loss.*

The blade of Li-Po's sword was large enough to be a mirror…. for fools; it was the weight of the blade and its shape that made it the sword worthy of a master swordsman, which he was.

One night, it was Li-Po and Rabbit who sat on that rock. The poet was again looking down at the moon as the pond had chosen to present it. He said aloud, but perhaps he was not speaking to Rabbit, "The moon is calling to me. It is, I believe, an invitation. I think if it were not for this world (he looked up and around at the magical forest, which felt this look that took in everything and left nothing out) I would respectfully accept her offer."

This, too, yielded a tear from Rabbit, who sometimes – often – wished he didn't know what he knew, wished he couldn't feel what this miraculous man meant; but being the very personification of Nature as Li-Po was, how could Rabbit not know?

Rabbit said, half-dismissingly, "The moon can wait. She knows where she can find us when the time is right. But this," Rabbit was pressing his luck here and he knew it, "But this isn't the time." If he had to explain why this wasn't the time, he couldn't do so. Such explanations simply do not exist; they're all made up; they're all contrived; invented; created with the best of intentions. The moon knew this, too; that's why she let it slide.

*Editor's note: The first poem is written by Li-Po. The second, by T.A. Young pretending to be Li-Po.*

# 6

# Elephant and Rabbit and Skib Redux

Elephant, Rabbit, and Skib were headed to a little party celebrating the birth of some kid, when they were waylaid by a man who appeared to be older than the mountains. His grey beard practically swept the ground before his feet, yet his eyes were clear and sharp and, if you had to guess, had seen everything in creation: the storm blasts and the land of ice; water that burned "like witches' oils"; the Spectre woman, and far, far worse.

It isn't about how long you've lived; it's about how much you've seen. What you have seen.

This old man, cursed like Cassandra, had seen it all.

Elephant asked his name. "Call me....

Ishmael.... No, I borrow that from another sea dog. Saved by a coffin, he was. Of a friend. The coffin was empty, the friend swallowed by the sea." He grew pensive. "Not so different. He, too, ol' Ishmael, has seen more than he should. Yes, you can see too much. Long-winded old tar. Not just seeing, you see, but *understanding* what he saw. It's both, you know, that matter."

Elephant turned to Rabbit, as usual, for translation.

Rabbit said very quietly, "We are in the presence of great magic. The greatest magic."

Elephant said, "I had that feeling."

"Funny, they call me 'loon.' I know what they mean, of course: the moon *has* changed me. No doubt, no doubt. But a loon, too: that solitary, sad bird whose nourishment comes from the sea. Divers, they are, and they are named for their melancholy utterances, for they are quite, quite alone. Almost a cry, I would say. Though sometimes I think both are befitting bynames for such as I."

He looked straight ahead as if he were seeing the vasty ocean, making him quiet as the rock that held him. Then he resumed: "If you could see the weight of the world; if you could see what complete vision looked like; if you could see a man who carried too much and saw too much and knew too much…but you can't: none of us can. 'Hold off! Unhand me, grey-beard loon!' says he. And yet, the wedding guest was touched, even by the slightest snip of dust or sea salt – cursed, perhaps – and made "A sadder and wiser man." All are thus touched. I ask you, I ask myself, am I a blessing or curse? Am I blessed or cursed? Who dares crush a man on his wedding day? A day of inebriation, not of such somber sobriety?"

Wisdom is no blessing. Immortality, too, is no blessing; ask Cain, or Utnapishtim, or the souls on the Flying Dutchman.

Rabbit asked, "Sir, what can we do for you? I mean, to make you comfortable. I mean, your story, the albatross and all, the stillness of the sea, the mist and ice and you…your….and death and death…the hermit!"

"Sir, you know the story. You know, too, that I am now bidden to tell my tale."

Rabbit said, "'I pass, like night, from land to land; I have strange power of speech.'"

The old sailor smiled, "We are kindred souls, you and I, and I think our friend there is such as us." He nodded in the direction of Skib, who had uttered not a syllable.

"It is a terrible burden, at times, to tell our tales. To teach. But we have been chosen, or our actions have chosen us, I know not. Nonetheless, it is our task to tell and teach. The world – you three know better than most – the world is a vaster place than we can ever know. Even my eyes do not tell the entire story, though I am told they give some intimation of all that is yet we cannot see."

Skib liked being the note-taker, the scribe for the magical forest. The responsibility, certainly, was great; yet the pleasure of enjoying the goings-on and the words in a double way – first, seeing and hearing them, then putting them to paper – it was a double pleasure. And he too felt that he was escaping time; the events and the words passed, but the ink on the paper remained. He felt he was cheating time, or at least abetting all those happenings that would otherwise be victims of time. If he did not remind himself that he was a truck driver, he would have allowed himself to feel heroic. Like a victor of something. He shrugged at these 'deep' thoughts; wheel and clutch and accelerator and brakes and solid lines and broken lines and yield signs and stop signs and traffic lights and cargo in and cargo out and gas stations and diners and home and away and home and away and his woman – he was lucky – his woman who was there for him: he had to remember all this, for this was his life, too, no more, no less, by any measure.

And would the life of the mariner be so different? Would he forget – ever – the foremast and mainmast and jib and bowsprit and shrouds and cabins and wheels and booms and decks and spars and yards and fore and aft? These were not in his blood; these *were* his blood.

Skib was not a new man, but he certainly was not

the same man. He would write what he saw and he thought he was thinking – or supposed to be thinking – as he wrote. Now, he wondered if he was supposed to be thinking or just noting, just reporting what he saw. Just then he saw……

Carl the ant walked up the rock. Or did he just walk? Or was he running? And is rock enough? Does it have to be a rough rock? Does it matter what rock? Who is he writing for?

Does Carl, the rock, or the roughness of the rock matter? Should we ask Carl? Who decides? With this, the first image Skib happened upon with his newfound knowledge and responsibility came the gravity of getting it right, whatever 'it' is. Whether the rock is the mover or the moved or unmovable, it is that damn rock that alludes to Sisyphus, and that is what we all have to move, be moved by, or just resign ourselves to. Does the roughness of the rock matter? This is one tough question for Skib and for all of us.

The old sailor sat on what the magical-forest folk called Daryl's Rock, so called because Daryl the crow called it his home away from home, which was a glorious oak not far away, but far above. The sailor let his hands enjoy the rough texture of the rock. Solid. Firm. He wondered if the sea had failed him or quite the opposite.

The three creatures watched the fourth. Boy, he sure was a study in pensiveness.

Elephant whispered as if he were in a church, "What is he?"

Rabbit asked, "What do you mean?"

"I mean is he sad or lonely or maybe confused. Lost, I mean."

Rabbit, too, was whispering. "That's a toughie."

The mariner said something.

Rabbit asked, "Did you say something?"

"My heart burns," he said. He raised himself from the rock. "I have to move on."

Elephant's heart felt pain. "You can stay with us!" He practically yelled this. "Stay with us! You'd like it here. You'd have friends!"

The old sailor smiled and patted the Elephant on his leg. Then he shook the paw of Rabbit and the hand of Skib, and said, "I hope I am allowed to return, someday. Thank you." And down the path he went.

"What did he mean, 'Allowed'?" Elephant wiped away a tear with his trunk. He felt sad and frustrated. "Who's in charge here!"

Rabbit and Skib felt the same way. Rabbit said, "I don't know, my friend, but if it's the same power that brought you down the river to me, and brought Skib down the road to us, and the knight, and all the others… There are good things, too."

The three of them sat on the ground simultaneously and looked at Daryl's Rock.

It stayed quiet for a long time.

As the sun slid behind the trees, Elephant broke the silence: "Red ducks?"

Skib wondered if he should include Elephant's featherbrained mondegreen in his scrivening, much less as the capper for such a weighty story. He wondered if his duty was to accuracy or to some responsibility to his reader. Was he supposed to write True stories or Good stories; Honest stories or Powerful stories? We mean, should he have to choose? Both are always best, but "Red Ducks"? Is that the way you want to end the story of the man who bore the weight of the albatross? And what is our responsibility, our debt to this member of a divine elect? Skib wished for the days when he could just jot things down and let the reader pull them all together, make stories out of them. So much easier, then.

Skib re-read what he had written. We leave him with his pen suspended above the page.

# 7

# Nullibiety

Some day, someone should do a study of how a rabbit and an elephant can be equally quiet. There they sat, either immersed in or devoid of thought; there was no way you could tell from the outside. But immobile and, judging from their mugs, untroubled. Let us pause for a moment of envy. We've seen similar faces on the subway during either rush hour, but only similar; those faces are immobile, but usually the result of utter exhaustion, the kind that goes with complete surrender to one's crappy treadmill days and the miserable acceptance that tomorrow – by definition – will be precisely the same. The pain that surpasseth understanding.

But what if this is some kind of wild metaphor

for the theme of this story? What if Rabbit Silence = Elephant Silence because Silence is Silence. Whose Silence it is does not matter. Not like Shadows. Elephant's Shadow does not equal Rabbit's Shadow even though both are Shadows. Whether Shadows are the result of or examples of or conditions of or states of Presence or Absence, we shall soon have to consider. Tell us that Shadows are merely the absence of light given the penumbra or parameters or contrasts or the result or conflict of some extra/external/exterior physical entity that is compatible or otherwise with some other entity called Light.

What Light is shall be approached as soon as we can muster the nerve to do so.

Rabbit scooped up something in his paw and was fiddling with it.

"What did you find?"

"Oh, nothing. A piece of nothing."

Elephant flipped. "A piece of nothing? A piece of nothing? How....I mean....I can't even find a whole nothing – which should be easier because it's bigger....I mean, it's a whole, entire Nothing! And you found a little piece of Nothing? You really are Rabbit!" Boy, was he filled with admiration.

"Where is Somewhere?" asked Elephant.

"Everywhere is Somewhere."

"Then, where is Nowhere?"

"I don't know. I've been around and I've always been Somewhere. But I've never been Nowhere. I've heard about it, but no one seems to be able to tell me – or want to tell me – where it is. I don't know if they're trying to protect me or help me or if they're hiding something: like, if there's a reason for keeping the location of Nowhere a secret. Though, of course, it's possible, they're making it up, this Nowhere place or thing or whatever it is. We should talk to someone about this. Someone who really knows what's out there....or not out there." Rabbit laughed to himself, enjoying his cleverness. Just a chuckle, really.

"You mean, it isn't here? Or maybe just around here somewhere?"

"Funny. You'd think of all the places for Nowhere to be, this would be a good location for it. I mean, if you wanted to tuck it away somewhere, we certainly have the space for it. But I just haven't seen it."

"Who do we ask?"

"Whom."

"Who is Hoom? Is that a wizard or something?" That "Hoom" sound raised a lot of ears, not for grammatical reasons (do you know how many magical-forest creatures care about the difference between subject pronouns and object pronouns? The same number that care *outside* of the magical forest: nine), but for the sound. (And do you know how many creatures care about if and when to use commas with parentheses? Yep: nine. But we're drifting, here. As opposed to drifting here, but that's for those nine knuckleheads.

But that sound – "Hoom" raised the specific ears of Rabbit and Elephant – which is truly impressive ear-raising, given these critters defining qualities – and they ran to either side of Skib who had just written "Hoom."

"But why not '"Whom'?" asked Rabbit.

Skib said, "I had to try to be faithful to the situation. To Elephant's ear. I had to take a big liberty and write what I thought Elephant was hearing, not the spelling of it. I could have been wrong." Skib looked at Elephant to get a read on this. Elephant nodded his head and said, "Yep, that's how I heard it," which was an important affirmation for the magical-forest transcriber. Or transcriber of the magical forest, which, when phrased that way, sounds really heavy.

Skib added – and this was all sincerity (he is not the pretentious type) – "I try to capture the essence."

Because they were still looking over his shoulder, they reacted to that line, which you, dear reader, can categorize as words written, spoken, both, or neither. *Bonne chance*!

Rabbit was not partial to that phrase: "Capture the essence. Really? Who the heck says 'capture the essence'?"

Elephant asked, "What does that mean?"

Rabbit said, "Skib's saying he tries to get the gist of what's going on, and then he tries to put it in that notebook. And ask me what 'gist' means. I will literally run into a burrow and have all my meals delivered."

What made him so crabby so suddenly is open to speculation. And who says, 'open to speculation' anyway? The same creatures who say, "capture the essence" and "superlative application of Baroque ornamentation to moderate the augmented caesuras."

"Listen, before we go on, do you know what Time is?"

"Well, I guess maybe it's around dinner time, the way the sun is looking, now. Like the moon, I mean. Orange and all but not so it hurts your eyes. And the way it's slipping behind the trees and all. Also, my stomach."

Rabbit is no saint, but he was really scoring points in heaven's ledger, today. "No," he said with nary a clenched jaw, "no, not if you know what time *it* is, but what Time is. Capital T."

Elephant had to think for just a moment before deciding that the answer was Yes. "Yes," said he.

"Good. I think you do, too. The problem is, if you had to describe it. If you had to tell someone what it is."

"You're right! But do you want me to try? Give it a shot, as you would say."

"Why not? Go for it."

Elephant looked left and right, up and down, as if searching for the answer. Then he said something so provocative, Rabbit wished he had a notebook (but then he realized Skib was taking notes like a crazed journalist). "Time," said Elephant, "isn't Nothing. The reason I know that is that it holds so much. It's like the biggest box ever that everything goes in. Maybe it goes in after we've used it, or maybe it's already in the box and we take everything out of the box, but in a certain way, or maybe we're all in the box together. But I would say it's the box that holds Everything. That's my answer."

Rabbit was rapt. "How...." He could hardly find the words: "How…?" Nope: he was too mesmerized to formulate a response, so he just sat there unconsciously gripping the little bit of nothing that he still held. Was there a connection? Or should we say, 'Is there a connection?' because if we—if *Everything* – is in the same box – not *was*, not *will be*, but IS – then the connection should still be in there…..Unless someone took it out, of course. But then, is it now WAS just because it was taken out of the box? And isn't the Past—*especially* the Past—still in the box? Doesn't it have to be?

"Can there be a Place without Time?" continued Elephant. "A Time without Place? I mean, if there is Something, there has to be a place for it. It has to be in a Place. Can there be Something that is Nowhere?"

"Wait a minute, wait a minute. You're going too fast."

This last statement astounded Elephant who thought it would be impossible for him to go too fast for Rabbit. Especially Rabbit, who was renowned for his quickness.

"There is someone we could ask about all this: Tumash."

"Who is Tumash?"

"Tumash The Bear. She's a genius. She's read, like, everything ever. And she's a practicing Offthepath. She has degrees and everything."

Elephant said, "Wow!" convincingly despite having no idea what an Offthepath is. Rabbit knew this, but the effort was good enough for him. That's friendship.

She's from Heron Inn."

"Here on in...what?"

Tumash was lying on her belly, with her head on her chin. "Ah, this is a matter – a conjecture, conundrum, paradox, the mystery, really, – that has been troubling us for millennia."

Elephant corrected her: "Actually, it just came up a couple of minutes ago. Before that, we were alright." She ignored him.

"The Greeks..."

Elephant broke in again: "How come whenever we ask stuff, someone brings up the Greeks. Who the heck are The Greeks? I mean, obviously by the name, they're some kind of lizard, but how do they seem to know so much?"

Rabbit did his impersonation of a block of cement, waiting for Tumash to mentally swat Elephant's words away, and continue. "The Greeks," she resumed, "....Of course, the metaphysical solipsism pre-exists the epistemological solipsism." She turned to Elephant and said, "Take Zero, for example...."

"But isn't Zero *Nothing*? How do you take Nothing? Is that *doing* anything? Is that *taking* anything?"

"Good questions. So, if you take Nothing, what do you have?"

"Nothing."

"So, do you or do you not have Something, and this Something is called Nothing."

"But I didn't take anything! I didn't move a muscle. So how did I end up having Anything?"

"Excellent," said Tumash. "So, in your opinion - in your world, your cosmos, your creation, your invention, your perception – would you say Zero is a number? Can you, for example, count to Zero? If you have zero eggs in a basket, do you have a basket of eggs?"

"No."

"Would it be fair to say that a basket of zero eggs is precisely the same as a basket of zero planets? Would they be equal?"

"No," said Elephant, "Because the basket might have zero eggs but seven planets, or some other thing, like lunch."

"But here is one of our problems: what are our *terms*? Are we saying quote basket or quote basket of eggs or quote basket of zero eggs? Try this: are quote *you* AN Elephant, THE Elephant, A Whooshponder, AN or THE Elephant who arrived here with Rabbit, and so on. What is the *term* for YOU? How do we *define* YOU? It's the same problem as the basket." Tumash paused. She knew a saturation point when she saw one, and she smiled benevolently.

Skib was forced to interject, which he had wanted to do much earlier. "Excuse me, but is that…" (he was reading from his notebook) "Is that METAP FIZZICLE or METAF HIZOCAL?

Rabbit answered for her: "We can check for the spelling, later. You're close enough."

"But I'm the writer," said Skib. You could hear the pain in his voice. "It's literally my job to get this all down, to write it the way it's meant to be! I can't just make things up to fill in the blanks!"

Tumash thought this was hilarious; not the plaintive-voiced part, not the intensity, not the sincerity, but the absurdity – the innocent absurdity – "My goodness," she thought, "it is so beautiful!" And she meant this sincerely.

Skib had more questions. "So, I mean, is being no place the same as being in Utopia? Doesn't Utopia mean nowhere or no place? So, is that good? Utopia, I mean. I know when that guy wrote the book, it was supposed to be a real place, but not a place that could ever be or that you could ever get to, but if you were there, would that be Nullibiety?"

Tumash said, "Certainly, but it could be called anything and the point would remain. Don't let the names—they're *just words*, Skib—I'm sorry because I know this is how you define yourself—but just words. Imagine if we had two separate words for shadows, one for shadow as presence, one for shadow as absence. Let's say, the former is Phenomenon and the latter is Noumenon. We can even justify this by saying, that the absence is pure intellectual intuition, and the presence is a real, tangible, solid. Stand in it. Stand *under* it, this shadow, and you can experience it. And what about Shade? Is that different?"

Skib was torn: How can someone like Tumash say "just words" or "mere words" when she used them so well and knew so many and, worst of all, made all these words into something so deep and beautiful and baffling. He loved his task more than ever. He said to her, "You know what? I love my task more than ever! Just words! That's like saying a painting is *just* paint or music is *just* sounds! You make them—words, I mean—*something*! I mean, You!"

Tumash blushed. She smiled and said, "This is from John 6:12 and I'm quoting, here: 'Let nothing be wasted.' Yes, I'm quoting out of context, but the sentiment....I repeat this line to myself often....the gorgeous ambiguity... 'Let nothing be wasted.'

Waste nothing? How do you waste Nothing? Yet, those are the instructions." Tumash closed her eyes and lifted-off (metaphorically) out of the forest and off the planet and—let's be conservative—into the mesosphere.

Elephant asked Rabbit, "So, what happens now? Do we know the answer? Is Nothing Something?"

Rabbit said, "There's this guy, Plato, and what he says is, there is no Nothing. Even when we're born....even before we're born.....we're loaded with knowledge and all kinds of stuff from past lives....I know, I know: past lives...but his point is, there is no Nothing. Nothing is just the stuff we haven't remembered yet."

Elephant didn't say anything. Rabbit used the silence to think, then he said, "At least, I think that's what he said. Plato. It might be a soul thing. Anyway, Plato."

Elephant said, "Did you know that Elephants never forget?"

Rabbit said, "Son of a gun! You know, I heard that, Elephants never forget. Ain't that Something!"

Skib was exasperated: "So, why am I writing all of this down?"

We pause to ponder. Then we hear the answer:

Rabbit said, "Because writing and remembering are not the same. Unless you're a court stenographer, they aren't meant to be the same. You don't put the image of a tree on a canvas to remember what a tree looks like; you do it for different reasons. Better reasons. You think god said, "I better put all of this down on that planet I just created in case I forget something?

"He was doing a little thing I like to call 'Creation.' There is always – always! – a difference between what is in your head and what ends up on that canvas. Buck up! Excelsior! Where are the snows of yesteryear! That's all I got for now."

# A few words from the... author?

I first met Rabbit at the All-In Truck Stop on Interstate 95 on the outskirts of Las Vegas. This diner had already become a special place for me, for it is where I met Biff Wellington, the fellow who literally dropped *The Fairy Tale Book*\* into my hands a year earlier. I did what Wellington asked—or didn't ask, I'm still not sure—and had it published, giving him full credit for those stories, more than half-hoping he'd get in touch with me again when he saw it. It may still happen. Whenever I'm sitting in the diner, I get the feeling I'll see him.

The thing about Wellington (and then we

\**The author refers to* The Fairy Tale Book *of Bifford C. Wellington* promise we'll get to Rabbit) is that he was all about the road. Or roads. He knew so much about roads, he even knew when it was time to get away from them. Some roads give and some roads take. He reminded me of the knight who passed through often, having a terrible time getting comfortable on a stool at the counter. He was tired, too. He left his horse by one of the pumps; that old gray wasn't what he used to be. But what is? Who is? As old and gray and worn as he was, he didn't look like he was finished, on his last legs, like his journey was over. That gaunt old knight had many, many miles left in him, and his horse would never fail him.

One day, the knight would pass, perhaps in battle, perhaps in his sleep, and his horse—his steed—noble to the end, would stand over his body, guard him, give his obsequies, then would lie down, himself. Because of where we are and who we are and where he is and who he is, we can tell you with absolute confidence that this horse would receive his worthy obsequies, too, from the birds and squirrels and grass and flowers and trees around him, for nature receives its own gladly and warmly and in nature nothing dies, but simply changes.

So, I was sitting in my favorite booth, the one I was sitting in when I first met Wellington, the one I always grab when Frog isn't sitting in it, when Rabbit comes in. He came right over, which for some reason

I expected he would do, though both his coming over and my expectation were completely inexplicable. And if that isn't the point of this entire story, I don't know what is.

Anyway, I slid into the booth and the waitress, Tracy, was right there to hand me a menu. She came back with a glass of water and told us to take our time. Rabbit said, "I like the vibe of this place. Hard to believe The Aladdin is just an hour away. Except for those slot machines." Rabbit nodded in the direction of the slot machines.

It may have been Rabbit's first question that made me like him right away: "You know the difference between noumenon and phenomenon?"

"The Kant thing?"

"See? I knew this was the right booth." He sipped his water and glanced at the menu.

"The waffles look good." Rabbit paused. "That's a funny thing. What makes something look good on a menu? It's just words…on paper, for heaven's sake. But, waffles it is!"

I thought to myself, "This is some rabbit." Then I considered the fact that I knew exactly zero other rabbits, so this rabbit may actually be a less impressive rabbit; I really have to get out more.

"Good choice." I figured I should wait for Rabbit to follow up on the Kant thing.

He ordered coffee, orange juice, the waffles.

I waited. Outside, an eighteen-wheeler came

between the diner and the desert.

Rabbit said, "You know what's great about these diners?" I hoped this was going to lead us back to Kant.

Rabbit continued, "What's great about these diners is they're timeless. I mean in the sense that you can order breakfast for dinner, dinner for breakfast, you can eat at four in the afternoon or four in the morning....Other places make these rules about when you can eat what – or is that, what you can eat when? – anyway, they're silly rules. Arbitrary. You know what I mean? Not all rules..."

The eighteen-wheeler pulled out leaving an unobstructed view of another eighteen-wheeler. Rabbit saw it, too, and said, "Ha! Reminds me of the first time I saw Elephant. Talk about your eighteen-wheelers. You know."

I did. Don't ask me how.

The waffles came and Rabbit doused them with syrup. He called Tracy over and asked if she could put a little whipped cream on them. She got the can and made a creamy pyramid, looked at Rabbit for his approval, didn't get it, so she doubled it.

Rabbit said, "How about if I say 'when'?"

Tracy looked at me and said, "Who knows, he may be a good tipper." She shrugged and the waffles soon disappeared under the avalanche.

He sank in and it must be said he looked enormously happy with all that whipped cream on his mug.

"Don't worry, I didn't forget about Kant. Give me a minute."

"No rush." I meant it. I loved this place, so any excuse to linger worked for me.

### ...and a word from Rabbit

Sometimes I need a little fresh air. Who doesn't? So, when I need a break from trees and flowers and streams and the incessant babble of numberless creatures of every ilk yakking about why one branch is better than another or one lily-pad is better than another or one rock....you get the idea....I hike up my hide and head out for my favorite getaway: the All-In Truck Stop on Interstate 95 on the outskirts of Las Vegas. It's a remarkably short trip for me to get from the magical forest to the diner of the All-In; it's like half a turn through a revolving door.

# II

*To the Diner - And Beyond*

# 1

# The Night Manager, Misunderstood

Skib and Rabbit were at their usual table. It was dawn. A young woman walked in, very thin, wearing dark blue work clothes that were far too large for her frame. Embroidered over the left pocket were the words "Operations Manager." She slid into a booth and Tracy was there in a flash to pour her a cup of coffee. Her hair was black in a loose ponytail; her skin white; her sleeves rolled up, revealing tattoos on both forearms. She added nothing to her coffee, gazed absentmindedly at the menu, studied the palms of her hands…in short, she had no idea what to do. When she wasn't working, she was adrift.

Skib asked, "Who is she?"

"She's the night manager."

"Then why is she coming in first thing in the morning?"

"What?"

"Why is she coming in to work now?"

Rabbit got it. "She isn't coming in to work; she just got off duty. She's the night manager."

Skib didn't get it. Rabbit said, "She doesn't manage the diner; she manages Night. Her shift just ended."

"Wait. Wait. What are you....? What do you mean...?"

This is why Rabbit describes himself as a saint when it comes to patience. He would take a deep breath, remind himself that he should not presume that his audience knows bupkis about anything, and then explain in the slow cadence of a person who is trying very hard not to pull his ears off out of frustration.

"You see," said Rabbit, "she's in charge of Night. These things do not run by themselves. They need oversight and occasionally a little tweaking, even the occasional pulling of a switch or rearranging of furniture."

"Can I talk to her?"

"Why not? But she ain't coming to you. Do you want me to walk you over, introduce you? It's probably a good idea."

So, over they go.

"Regina."

"Rabbit."

"Mind if we join you for a minute."

Regina gestured to sit down.

"Regina, this is Skib."

"The note-taker."

"Yeah. He has a couple of..."

She looked at Skib. "Shoot."

Regina looked about twenty-five in human years. She had a complexion so perfect, it was distracting.

"How long have you been...."

"I've been the night manager since the beginning. The only one." She smiled. "I've been doing this for eternity plus one. I have one day's seniority over the day manager. And by day, I mean countless, measureless, indivisible, unsegmented, unrelenting, rolling exponentially-multiplied eons, as you would call it. That's just to be clear. But some would argue that it all really begins with the time card." She waved Tracy over and asked for a slice of sweet potato pie.

"Now you're going to ask me what I do, exactly. The answer is, I do everything exactly. I can't get anything wrong, timing-wise or place-wise or size-, density-, speed-, gravity- or anything else-wise. It's like that Buddhist joke: a monk asks Buddha, 'What is the perfect question and what is the perfect answer?' Buddha responds: 'That is the perfect question, and this is the perfect answer.' Most of the time, things run pretty smoothly on their own, but once in a while you can have a mess to deal with." She smiled again. "See all this?" She made a small circle with her teaspoon - "Some say 'Dharma.' Some say 'a screw-up. What is was never meant to be.' How's that for a paradox? You let one little comet nudge one little asteroid into one mass of until-then meaningless mass of rock and everything changes. We had to reorganize the whole system. Luckily, it had exactly no impact on the rest of the universe. Hey, it happens."

Tracy brought over the pie. "Anything for you guys?"

Rabbit said, "The pie looks good. Can we get a couple of slices?"

"You're getting the last of it, you lucky ducks. Sorry. You know what I mean."

# 2

# Frames

E lephant was looking at a painting on the wall of the diner.
"I don't get it."

Rabbit looked at it and asked, "What don't you get?"

"Where's the rest of it?"

"The rest of what?"

"Everything that isn't in the little box." Elephant outlined the frame with his trunk.

"Okay, that's not a box, it's a frame. It goes around the picture."

"But it chops off everything. Look, half a boat, half a tree, half a lake...you know there are more birds over there….You know there's more stuff up here, closer to us…." His trunk was moving all over the place.

"There are limits."

"Limits?"

"Where," asked Elephant, "Where are the limits? I've never seen one."

"You know. Like when we go down to the river. There's the dry part, then there's a line – sort of - ….." (Ever have an explanation turn into vapor even as you're saying it?) "….sort of. Then, uh, there's the wet part. The river. So, the limit would be that line….."

"But that's not a limit, that's Another. You know, Another Thing. They're connected. Always. Everything." Elephant had no intention of being the embodiment of Eastern Philosophy; he was just calling it the way he saw it. Clarity.

Rabbit thought, then said, "I got nothin'."

"And what if there were limits? Couldn't the box be made a little bigger to let in more of the important stuff?"

"Maybe the artist thought all the important stuff was already in there? What if he wanted you to really focus on just what he stuck in the frame?"

Elephant raised his right foot. Rabbit said, "Don't even think about it. You'll bring the whole place down. You want to have a tantrum, do it outside." Elephant gently lowered his leg.

"Why do humans have to frame things? Put boxes around everything? It's like they make stuff to deliberately get in the way of things. Like rooms and houses and lines. Lines make me crazy. You know who else hates lines? Ants. Ants hate lines. You know why? Because someone keeps making them walk in lines. How would you like to have to walk that way?"

"Don't Whooshponders walk in lines?"

"Wooshponders don't walk in lines; they just like to follow each other. We take up a lot of space, so that's the easiest way to move around. But never lines! If there's a line, that's someone's brain imagining things."

"Okay, okay. Let's go back to the forest and walk in circles for a while. You'll feel better."

Elephant already felt better just thinking about his non-linear, non-liminal world.

When they got back to the forest, Elephant was almost giddy. Cheech The Mole turned to his cousin and said, "That elephant looks drunker than a bee."

His cousin said, "That would make one happy bee."

As Rabbit tried to keep up with Elephant's insult to Terpsichore without being squashed, he tried to speak profoundly about the cause of their little tiff, to wit: frames.

# 3

# Frames versus Palimpsests

"**F**rames," Rabbit began, assuming with great confidence and inexcusable misjudgment that Elephant was listening, "frames….are certainly an issue. I mean, I get what you said about how they seem to cut off the rest of the picture, which is not the way it works. In real life, the thing that cuts off the rest of the picture is part of the picture. It isn't something else….like something from the outside. You and I….we know that there is no inside and outside when it comes to these things….we're all inside. Can you slow down a bit? Anyway, I think I have another idea for you to consider. Picture this: instead of frames, we say palimpsest." He paused waiting for the "What?" which he didn't get, which was not a good sign in the context of dialectic. He kept going anyway, being the Ahab of rabbit philosophers.

Skib had grown used to being the third wheel long ago, but being the visible third wheel was strange for him, running now to keep up with Rabbit and Elephant or trying to look nondescript sitting in an adjacent booth at the diner, his back to the pair, his baseball cap pulled low over his eyes, writing everything down in his notebook. The sunglasses were a little much.

For fun, Elephant would occasionally reach over Rabbit with his trunk and jostle Skib's cap, but Skib never turned around: he took his surreptitious role seriously, as absurd as it was. We can debate a) if this is an admirable quality, b) this is the comedic condition of mankind, c) this is the price of art, d) if this is what Boswell had to contend with. Suffice it to say, Skib's efforts to remain invisible had the opposite effect: trying not to be a character made him quite the character; hence, Elephant's playful spotlighting. It's the classic faux pax: "Pretend I'm not here."

# 4

# And Another Thing: A Dialogue

"And another thing." This was Rabbit.

"Do you think there are trees on the moon?" (This is called a fortuitous non sequitur, one of Elephant's signature qualities.)

"That's exactly my point. Follow me. You know what they call reality?" Rabbit was doing his Socratic thing.

"Yes. Not not real."

"Perfect. Not not real. So I'll give you two things and you'll tell me if they're real or not real."

"Then can we have lunch?" Elephant was nothing if not focused.

"Let's just finish the game. So, is the moon real?"

"Um....Yes?"

"Let's go with yes. The scientists tell us it's real.

Now how about a tree. Real?"

"Yessiree." Elephant loved the easy questions.

"So we have two reals. That'll be our label: reals. Now, if you ask 'Is there a tree on the moon?' you'd have to say no. The real tree and the real moon are not compatible. They cannot exist like that."

"So real is bad." Elephant was not as confident as he was with the tree question.

"We'll see. Now take the same moon, the real thing. And now we add a unicorn, the fakest, most unreal thing ever. No one, not here, not anywhere has seen a unicorn. Not real. So, how about a unicorn on the moon?"

"No."

"Same as the tree on the moon, am I right?"

"Yes."

"So, what have we learned?"

"Trees and unicorns cannot be on the moon." Elephant saw this was the conclusion he was supposed to reach.

"And what about reals and not reals?"

"It doesn't matter?" This is called thin ice. Imagine an elephant on thin ice.

"Precisely! It doesn't matter! So this thing that humans have been trying so hard to label, the real and unreal, to differentiate between the two, to argue that one is better than the other.....that's why they have so much trouble getting here." (He was referring to the magical forest). "Or sticking around once they're here. Do we have a gate here? A fence? Guards? A clock? An expiration date? But it ain't for everyone, I guess." (Pregnant pause.) "It makes you wonder, drawing lines - you'd say frames - when you don't need 'em."

"You know, I can just graze. I don't need anything fancy."

"You know that pun about Peter and the rock? That's an example of both: real and not real. He's a real rock, metaphorically speaking, and he's a metaphorical rock, metaphorically speaking, and he's the foundation, metonymically speaking, but he's not a literal rock even though he is literally the foundation, metaphorically speaking. You see what I mean?" Rabbit had been talking to himself since the word "graze" was spoken by Elephant. Sustenance is different for everyone.

---

"Deary," mumbled Elephant. (Under normal circumstances, 'deary' sounds nothing like 'Derrida,' but Rabbits – even with those ears – sometimes hear what they want to hear. We tell you this by way of the colossal misunderstanding that follows.)

"Criminy! You're right again! Derrida! The binary hierarchy! The metaphysics of Presence! That's the crux of the matter: We think that Presence is superior to Absence, even if it's the absent thing that yielded the present thing! Elephant, you've brought it perfectly full circle.

"Could we not just talk about this forever!"

## 5

# Between Rounds (The Fighting Kind, Not the Good Kind)

Skib had fallen asleep, notebook in his lap, pen nesting in his open hand. A bird would fly overhead or skim the surface of a pond. A frog would be startled at nothing and leap into the water and do the breaststroke. A flower would be reminded of the Vietnam War and begin singing Fortunate Son. Back at the diner, the knight was sitting at the counter, his shield slung behind him, eating a bowl of cereal.

The counter person, Nosmo King, who incidentally was the one who hired Tracy because they knew each other from high school, said, "For a knight on a quest you sure ain't makin' tracks."

"The going is slow at times. Wind, rain, ogres, rush-hour congestion, construction detours....those orange cones…..clearly the sign of the devil."

"But if you keep coming back here, how far can you get? I thought you guys moved in pretty much a straight line. Forward, I mean. How far can you get if you keep circling back?"

"What if the goal of my journey is here? Or very close to here? What if I am in no hurry to reach the end of my journey? What if I do not know what comes after the end? What if, and my experiences tell me this is quite possible, I am not here? Or why do I presume that this is always the same diner? Or what if the diner is coming with me on my journey?"

"Next time I'll stick to the weather."

"The funny part is, knights aren't supposed to be asking questions, I know. But then, Parsifal and all that. We are arrows directed at a goal by the divine archer called Destiny. Yet I find that the thing that I am aimed at - as if I really know what it is or what it means or why I must reach it and, having reached it, end my travels - is not as pleasurable as my movement through time and space. How can anything given the frightening name 'The End' be desirable?" The End seems a terrible place."

"Good points. More coffee?"

"What is your goal?"

The counter person (a name so loaded with meaning one has to ask if there was some intention in giving him such a title) filled the knight's cup and didn't rush into his answer. He was used to these challenges coming as they do from such a multifarious clientele. You want challenging questions? Talk to a mermaid seated at your counter in a diner in a truck stop in the middle of the desert. They just keep coming. The questions. The mermaids, too, actually. Go figure.

The counter person said: "My folks left me the house and it's all paid for. I've been pretty good with my 401k contributions. My wife, too. The kids are out and doing fine, so no need to worry about them. They'll get everything after we're gone. And you know, this is a cash business, so I have a nice bundle buried away; the years add up. No rush. No rush."

The knight said, "Ah, yes," though he understood about half of what the counter person had said.

"I suppose I'll know when I'm done. I hope so, anyway. I hope I don't get it wrong. I'm taking a little cigarette break. You need anything before I step out? Tracy's around, if you need anything."

It's a small world and a much smaller diner, so we shouldn't be too surprised that just as Nosmo stepped out through the back door, a dragon should walk in through the front. This entry was not easy: the dragon had to lower himself, scrunch himself, pull in his huge leathery wings, and otherwise contort himself to get through the double doors. Once in, or mostly in - curling his tail into what ended up looking like a pile of huge, scaly, green and yellow serrated truck tires - he took a seat or five at the counter, right next to the knight.

They looked at each other.

"George,' said the dragon with great civility.

"Ron," the knight replied, with equal equanimity.

"How are you holding up? I saw your horse outside. He's one tough cookie."

"We're both fine. Fine and fit."

"Seems you're both getting a bit long in the tooth."

The knight took his time to respond, "It wasn't so long ago. Should you choose for a rematch, we are up for it."

"Don't get your dander up, George. I'm just kidding around. You have no sense of humor. Where's the guy? I'm so hungry I could eat a mob of imbecilic villagers hoping to defeat me with bibles and pitchforks. Oh, for the days when they would practically run into my maw with that look on their faces. You know, that Greater-Good Expression? That always kills me."

"It will someday."

"Again, no sense of humor." The dragon turned his head. "Hey, hey Tracy!'

The dragon turned back to the knight. "Where to now?"

The knight said nothing, not to be rude or

provocative. Somehow, the dragon knew this. They were part of a fraternity; they were kindred spirits, imprecisely; they shaped, sculpted, literally carved each other. Their scars and their pains were part of what defined them. There is a beauty in this, even if the portraits are painted with swords and shields and claws and fangs and the bellowing of fire and the bending of armor and slashing of scales and utter indifference to mortality. After the non-answer, the dragon said with profound resignation, "I know the feeling."

# 6

# The Rig and the Gig

**S**kib Bricluster had a problem somewhat akin to the knight's, but perhaps we should have left that subtle parallel for the reader to discover, yielding an epiphany that would resonate in their - in your - spiritual being, enhancing the qualities within us that make us emanations to be reckoned with in this swirling, misty galaxy that is ironically the result of the crystalline entities that we call stars.

Why does it sometimes take so long to get to the point? Because that's the point. It's the getting to the point that is the point. Remember all that talk about journeys and quests and roads and paths and destiny and such? It's all coming together.

Yes, being the Magical Forest Archivist is rewarding and of immeasurable benefit to future generations, but there was a very large truck out there with Skib's name on it - literally - that should be loaded and unloaded and loaded etc. resulting in the ability to pay bills, which is a nice thing in this world, or this part of the world, or however you want to parse this planet.

The road beckoned. Rabbit beckoned. There was something impending. But the author - The Author! - wasn't sure what it was or was to be because of the whole volition issue, but we're getting a tad deep for this early in the story.

Skib made up his mind. (Volition issue #1) Then he made it up again. (Volition issue #2) As Skib stood by his rig, his forest pals watching, dabbing at tears as he filled the tank, he felt disoriented. The road looked long and straight; his truck looked big; for a second he wondered if he could get a leg up into the cab, even with the step. It had been a long while since he had to pull himself up. He did.

And then there was a silence that preceded the turn of the key. Then the sound of the engine, louder than he remembered. And the feeling of being alone. Commencing countdown.

How could he have made that choice? Did he really step on the pedal, shift into gear and lean on the accelerator? He looked into the mirror and half-watched - because he was a good driver - half-watched the diner recede in the dust.

And a great sadness descended on his world.

## A NOTE

(It should be noted that there is no rent in the magical forest. And mortgage rates are historically low, though there was that tenth-of-a-point bump just to test the waters. The waters typically respond negatively to these bumps, so they were quickly un-bumped. Don't mess with the Waters. We can talk more about this later, but remember, the Waters came first. Land was an afterthought.)

# 8

# Two Months Later

**(And the concrete temporality should be a clue)**

Two months later, Skib was unloading pressure board and plywood and, like good ol' Sisyphus, was feeling in the best way the weight of the wood, the pressure, the calluses under his gloves. He was again used to climbing into the truck, sliding the wood out, jumping down, laying it on the ground or the fork-lift or the arms of a fellow worker. He enjoyed the little cloud of dust that enveloped him like Pig-Pen's: it was always there. It was on him and in him and around him: an aura of dirt that he was actually proud of. Then home, to the shower, then to his sofa and television and refrigerator and microwave and wall-to-wall plush carpeting bought wholesale and laid-in by himself and his brother-in-law. Man, walking around in his socks on his plush carpet felt so good.

Skib met a gal who was divorced, had two kids, worked in the food court at the mall in Lindeburgh, who was a year older than he, but kept in shape, avoided the donut places and fried everything places and such, but was a sucker for ice cream, which is how they met, but that's a story that is so mired in love and romance, it is complete bereft of magic. She - Abigail Kolaizcek - would disagree despite seeing love come and go like seasonal allergies; she thinks love is magic, though the evidence is scant and dubious. Skib, having actually seen magic, knew better. Not that he derided love, but magic it was not.

So she moved in, Abigail did, to the wall-to-wall plush carpeted heaven that was Skib's two-bedroom ranch with partly-finished basement, which means couch, rug and big-screen television. The kids shared their bedroom and thought they, too, were in heaven because they'd been living with her sister's family for a year and that meant crowded rooms and sleeping bags and taking a number to use the bathroom. Here, they had their own beds and closets. The trick to having happy kids is to let them see the contrast with other lifestyles. No, not see, but experience.

But there was a problem and the name of that problem was Skib. The absurdity – nay, illogicality -

of that foregoing statement can neither be exaggerated nor overstated. And that's what you call a bad sentence, but fun.

The problem was not Skib, but his creator, which has no intended theological implications whatsoever, so don't take it for more than it says.

He gave Skib too much depth. The history, the truck, the house, and now Abigail. Poor Abigail was just getting her footing after a lousy marriage to an unfaithful fireman, and now she had entangled herself with a work of fiction, practical as he may be. To Rabbit and Elephant, obviously; not Abigail. The wall-to-wall plush carpet was real; the bedrooms, real; Skib, nyet.

This goes back to our earlier discussion about the real and the unreal and whether they fit or not and so on. Here, they fit like a glove, but this fit does not fit with the reason for his creation. His raison d'etre. Literally. And for emphasis, we shall pronounce Literally in just three syllables, which oozes pretentiousness. Lit-ra-lly. Like a snob.

In the above paragraph we used the word - precarious, dubious, unreliable, non-specific - "Here." We hear you; we rise to the challenge of clarification: where, precisely, is Skib Bricluster? A question that has Multiple Choice written all over it. Okay:

*Elephant and Rabbit and Skib*

Where, precisely, is Skib Bricluster?

A. The All-In Truck Stop on Interstate 95
B. The Magical Forest
C. Cresslyn, Missouri
D. Rabbit's brain
E. Skib's brain
F. Bifford C. Wellington's brain
G. Bix Tinker's brain
H. Calliope's musings
I. Patrem Omnipotentem
J. Just the vowels

The correct answer is… Oh, I'm afraid we're out of time. Let's move on to the next room, shall we? The one where the women come and go, talking of Michelangelo.

# 9

# The Quandary Qontinued

Skib had stepped off the path, making us think of the night manager's words: he was drawn for the diner and the magical forest, and now he's in Cresslyn, Missouri. Let us take a moment to glare at his inventor and warn him not to do anymore freewheeling, irresponsible creating because he has a craving for an amanuensis. Melville did it right when he made Bartleby. Mary Shelley did it right. John Gardner did it right. Salinger did it right. It's called balance. Control. Keeping a leash on your creation, no matter how long the leash may have to be, as long as it's long enough to keep him/her/it in his/her/its world. And who has to pay for this? Yep, the creation. The creator gets to sit in her high-backed chair, ruminating, recriminating, ruing, doubting, as she sips her wine and admires her depth, while her creature has run off the map, also of the creator's making. So be it.

    Skib sat at the back of his truck with his legs dangling. He was one lost soul. The ubiquitous Rabbit (a now-erroneous epithet) was somewhere else, which is not where a central character is supposed to be, or without at least having some other character or narrator or author of for heaven's sake *whoever is in charge*, tell us where our central character is – meaning, it comes down to being either a matter of responsibility or trust between the reader and whoever is in charge here, and that when the adjective "ubiquitous" was chosen, it was either true or ironic, though, in the spirit of this text, we choose to believe it is true…in its own way And that, my friends, is deep. And that, my friends, is also why our editor takes Lexapro.

    Nonetheless, Skib sat looking like something Rodin dreamed up. Gopher was called in from the bullpen to replace Rabbit who was having a little soreness in his rotator cuff and his stats were beginning to wilt like Daphne The Butterfly's self-esteem when she turned three-hundred and thirty-six hours old, which to a mayfly, for example, would make a retirement plan a complete joke.

    Gopher was a smart character. He can use the words "deep," "chthonic," Plutonian" and metaphors like "roots" and "subterranean" and all that other "what lies beneath; what's buried; what cannot be seen; getting down to the heart of the matter"; and so on, because he spends a lot of time underground, but not to the point where he doesn't know what's happening above. Far from it. You can see the philosophical and spiritual advantages to this. Well, not see, but imagine. "See" is a tricky word when we're discussing gophers, who have very poor eyesight, but are loaded with insight. Not many people know this, but Tiresias was a gopher. Obvious now that we've said it. (N.B. There are other creatures with the same name.)

Gopher knew Skib from around the circuit. He asked him what was going on. Without thinking, Skib took out the notebook from his jacket pocket. It was so dirty and bent and creased and folded in, up, and over that it looked nothing like a notebook should. The pen looked pretty much like a pen. Once he was holding them, Skib realized a) he hadn't consciously taken them out and b) he had no idea if he wanted to use them. He wanted this conversation to be off the record. Yet here we are.

Let's give them their privacy and simply summarize in a respectful way the comeuppance, which is this: Skib didn't know what he was doing; where he was going; what he was meant to do; what the point was; where he was - really - that is to say, where he is. He didn't know what was important, anymore, if he ever did. He was a lost soul. Yes, we told you this earlier – the whole Rodin thing, but we just wanted to say it again, maybe so we can fit in something about Sartre or Camus or Kierkegaard or The Truman Show. "Where," he asked, "do I belong? And why?"

Gopher said, "What brings a lot of creatures to the Magical Forest is their lost souls. You and that notebook: you keep it for a reason, your own silly reason, but that's perfectly okay: I've seen more useless and cumbersome attachments." (*For the sake of verisimilitude – Really? In a text with dragons? – we note again that gophers have extremely poor eyesight, so when we use words that attribute vision to gophers, it should be read metaphorically or as synesthesia or supernal vision.*) "I'm not being all Haight-Ashbury psychedelic here, like, 'hey, man, this place could be anywhere'; I mean you have the choice of being anywhere. That's tough. That's why we gophers keep our tunnels simple: forward, backward and done. When you have no limits, you're a helium-filled balloon floating all over the place. Good luck finding a system, a pattern, a direction. Even 'up' doesn't do it. So, you need to ground yourself. You need to figure out where you want to be But, first you have to figure out what you want."

Tiresias The Gopher's words made Skib think about the cab of his truck, ringed with mirrors. It had dozens of maps on the passenger side, on the floor and the glove compartment. (A different time, no?) And he thought of soda cans and paper cups, a couple of rolls of paper towels, two bottled waters. He thought of the car radio. A lot of driving. Loading and unloading, and home. And, sure enough, the car behind him honked his horn: the light had turned green ten seconds ago! Let's go, man! He loved Joe Cocker. Exit 23, then stay to the right. His girlfriend would be home from work; she was an assistant-something somewhere, but moving up. Does this guy know how to work a directional indicator? He hit the brakes. Gopher laughed: "You creatures crack me up. I think you humans were created to annoy each other. C'mon."

Skib knew Tiresias was right. He knew what he needed and no, the answer is not a Rabbit hole (though how fitting would that be!) and it wasn't a mirror you could step into, or astral directions from Peter Pan. Skib had been on this road before and knew the perfect exit: Exit 43, Iron Mountain. The parking lot was not built for eighteen-wheelers, but it was a piece of cake for Skib to neatly fit in. Stepping down from the cab, he already felt better. Closer. He and Tiresias followed a trail that led to the woods himself up to the top, then turned exactly 87 degrees and headed up a small hill. Son of a gun if there wasn't a rock that looked familiar. He pulled himself up to the top, closed his eyes and heard his friend's voice ask, "Where's your notebook?" They were back in the Magical Forest.

Gopher volunteered to retrieve it, which he did, but not right away. A young woman parked next to Skib's truck had seen him appear, climb, open the door, grab the notebook and so on, and was astounded. When Tiresias saw her look, he knew she was on to him. He muttered, "stupid notebook," and apologized to her for no reason whatsoever.

She spoke to him: "Are you some kind of trained animal? Like some kind of trained secret agent or something? Are you a robot?"

"No, Sara, I'm not a robot. For crying out loud. And don't be surprised that I know your name. I know your whole story, including why you were sitting in your car in this parking lot. Anyway, the answer to your problem is not to move out. Work things out. Mike is a good guy. He will get his life in order and he will be the man he wants to be for you and for himself. So: sit tight. If you want to talk - I mean vent - just come here and sit on that rock and whisper - do not yell - my name, Tiresias The Gopher. I will hear you. You'd be amazed how close by I am. Are we good?"

"You speak English?"

"That's what you got out of what I said? I'm fluent in English! Don't be shocked when I tell you I speak every language on this planet. All of 'em. Anyway, just whisper "Tiresias" and I'll be here. Okay, gotta go."

Moments later, Skib had his notebook.

And, yes, Tiresias did hear Sara call out to him through Time and Space and Magic, "Thank you!"

(We won't say any more about their exchange because of that whole 'respecting their privacy' thing. It's called Integrity and we need lots more of it in this world. Especially this world.)

# 10

# An Abrupt Change of Venue

Skib was back at the diner in a trice, a term you don't hear often nowadays, so we'll define it for you: a trice is an extra-small booth that can hold two people if they are on the lanky side. Or one person if he or she is on the portly side. Or zero people if one or both are on the Falstaffian side. Skib liked its coziness and the fact that he didn't have to lean over to get his head over the plate. If he wanted, he could easily eat over the plate on the other side of the table, which was far leaner than the usual. He knew that Rabbit would have no problem with the seating, assuming he'd show up.

A Trice is also a vehicle drawn by a horse and pulley that gets you practically nowhere. It was invented by Gillard Palanquin in 1757 in Barouche, Wisconsin for Fleetman Brougham, land baron and pain in the ass. Palanquin's vehicle was a complete disaster, causing whiplash in its riders, much to the joy of Brougham, who knew better than to set foot into that three-wheeled affront to vehicular progress (hence the confusion with the Thrice, another three-wheeled gem, invented by Quill Maskeep.) What this block of information should convey to you is that we're killing time until Rabbit shows up to join Skib. [***To my editor:***This is frigging hysterical: how can you delete this!]

While we were clawing our way through the slough of authorial despond above (*The despond is the author's—whoever that is—the result of his anxiousness, uneasiness, and loneliness resulting from his having to wait until Rabbit shows up. - T.A. Y*) (***Editor:*** *This stays in? Like this? Not bad!*), Skib had taken out that notebook and started jotting an idea he had for a poem. His first. Here it is:

> Sitting here I see
> Carl the Bee.
> Hello, Carl,
> What's your name?
> It's Carl, Skib,
> What's your name?
> It's Skib, Carl,
> Can you stay a while?

No, said Carl,
I have to buzz.
And so he does.

Skib re-read it several times before crossing it out. Then he wrote this:

Hence loathed Melancholy
Bring me a beer and be gone
That Night may be supplanted by Light
Get off my lawn,
Let in the Dawn.

Then he got stuck and crossed that out, too. He looked around to see if there were any signs of our protagonist, but no. So, he gave it another try; he was enjoying the action, the writing of stuff; his own words, rather than everyone else's. And the physical part: the pen to paper. He let his pen glide around the page making flourishes, then stopping. He hadn't noticed the presence of the knight for we don't know how long. Short of forever, obviously, or we wouldn't have the part where Skib looked up, said, "Hello," and waved to the seat. The knight demurred because the fit would be a problem, but said, "Sir Skib, you are to join me. We are going."

"Where?"

"The Land of the Giant Hungry Serpents. But first, John The Smith, for my horse needs shoeing."

"Can I just go with you to the shoeing thing, and you can do the Land of Giant Serpents solo?"

"No."

"I'm sort of waiting...."

"Yes, waiting. You've mastered Waiting. You've made an art of it. You really know Waiting. Now, let's try something different, like battling Giant Hungry Serpents with impregnable skin; claws that can shred mountains; the speed and agility of panthers; and insatiable appetites. Never has a creature survived this test. Even the fabled Hercules ran like the wind after a few exchanges with these creatures."

"How many are there?"

"Hundreds. Luckily, they cannot swim, so they are corralled on their island. Theseus tried to bring one back to Athens, but it cost him twenty ships, one hundred men, and his left ear to find out that it wasn't going to happen. Are you ready?"

Skib closed the notebook and began to tuck it away when the knight stopped him. "You will need that."

"I don't think whacking a killer snake with a notebook is going to do much."

"It's to save this mighty, perilous, doomed battle for posterity. What is the point of perishing on an island of monsters, vanquishing perhaps one if we are very lucky, if no one will ever know about it. It must go into your journal. What a story it will tell!"

"Or," said Skib, "Or, what if I - we - just write up

the story like we'd like to imagine it and we save that for posterity? I mean, we don't have to be like major heroes or anything, just, like you said, maybe slay one snake, but we escape! We make our mark without the scar tissue or missing limbs. How about that? All legend, no risk!"

"That is the worst idea I have ever heard. It's dishonest. The truth is what makes it worthy of Posterity."

"No, it's the words that make it worthy. Like you said, we could die on that island up to our necks in truth, and without the words, no one would know. So much for truth. What you want is a story! And it isn't a lie, unless you make the title, 'Knight Slays Snakes: A True Story.' How many stories have that title? King Arthur: A True Story. Sir Gawain: A True Story. David and Goliath: A True Story. So, none. You're safe from hypocrisy."

"Excellent logic, Sir Skibney of Briclustershire." The knight then conked him on the head. "You are now duly dubbed. Our challenge awaits!"

"Ow." And they left.

Rabbit just missed them, so he worked on the crossword puzzle from yesterday's (talk about your useless words! Look up Deixis and prepared to be floored. No, prepare to be floored, then look up Deixis.) Fulton Spel, Oklahoma, Gazette.

## 11

# The Ironically Named 'Inviting Beach'

If there were a painting entitled, "The Inviting Beach," the Island of Giant Hungry Serpents could be its model. The lapping waves, the gentle breezes, the lulling sound of distant cataracts. A cataract is just another word for waterfall from deep within, teeming life invisible....the image literally kicks the viewer in the gut with its tranquility. Think of the Sirens, the sweet irresistible song of the temptresses., summoning you to be their dinner.

The knight and Skib disembarked from their single-sailed boat and dragged it to shore. They dropped the sail, picked up the tools of their trade, peered around and headed inland.

They came upon an enormous serpent, half coiled, its head rearing up when it sensed visitors. The knight drew his sword and stepped forward. Skib was already holding the sword lent to him by the knight, so all he had to do was take a step backward, a move that preceded another step backward, and that anticipated many more steps in that direction. Technically, it's called The Non-heroic Direction. Or katabasis, if you're Xenophon's second cousin.

The serpent hissed and the knight raised his sword.
"Who are you?" asked the serpent.
"I am the knight who is going to slay you."
"How come?"
"Sorry?"
"How come? Did I do something to you? Hurt your feelings or something? I've never seen you before, I don't think."
"We have just arrived on your shores. You are one of the Giant Hungry Serpents."
"I don't know about being giant serpents. We all seem to be about the same size, except for the little ones, of course. But they grow up. As for hungry, that's sure true. So, that's why you want to kill us? Don't all creatures get hungry?"
"Well...." The knight was stumped.
"I don't know, those don't sound like very good

reasons to me."

"Don't you want to kill us?"

"Will it make you feel better? Killing us, I mean. Like, should I attack you so you don't feel crappy about killing us.?"

The knight lowered his sword, turned and called to Skib who was several furlongs behind him. "This happens all the time. It's getting depressing. When did creatures - giant, scary creatures, no less - become so damn reasonable? Why am I the one who looks like the monster? I'm just trying to make myself worthy." He sat on the ground.

The serpent assumed this topic was still open for discussion. So, he said, "I'm no expert at this, but I'm pretty sure 'giant, scary creatures' have been reasonable since that - what do you call it? Moment? Kick-off? Starter's gun? - ah! since that very first quotation mark. Logos. Get it? I suppose that isn't the question. The question is, when did some creatures - ahem - run off the rails?"

This did nothing to motivate the knight to stand, so the serpent said, "Okay, let's do this; You take a few runs at me with your sword, I'll show my teeth and slam my tail, then you go home and all is well. Between us, I'm fine with this, because for you it's going to be like attacking a rhinoceros with a twig, but those are mere details. You can inflate as necessary."

The knight saw there weren't many options, so he

agreed. He turned to Skib and told him to get his notebook ready. Then the great battle began.

    This battle is brilliantly recounted in a multitude of texts in prose and poetry. Certainly, the contemporary works of Thordlyn Squireson and Madd Yels do a splendid job; their imagery is enthralling. The later writers, Karynna Thrudnbok, J. S. Phrilt, and Mault Lager should also be read. Lager, especially, brings the flour-sack-sized tonsils of the serpent, the gallons of spittle, and the steadfastness of the knight during what could pass for earthquakes with each slamming of the serpent's tail, very close to the realm of reality. What they all have in common is an almost innate reverence for the knight, creating - to borrow from the pantheon - from "a tattered coat upon a stick" "a form as Grecian goldsmiths make." If the knight were to see the statues built of him, he would self-consciously stand straighter. Again, it's the worthiness thing. Imagine having to measure up to your own legend? This is not a task for the meek. One must learn to tower. Ask Napoleon. ***Editor:*** *You are putting the battle in the past. Have Skib and the knight time-traveled? Or is there simply no linear time in the Magical Forest, if that's where the Giant Serpents lived? If there's no linear time, should this be brought out? It would be a good paragraph or two, yes?* ***T.A.Y.:*** *I like the idea of making the events "classic" and "historical." The readers will get it by the word (and context)*

of *"recounted."* But we could make this even more obscure...
**Editor:** Wait a bit. I need to refill my prescription.
***T.A.Y:*** Make it a double.

Skib's notebook, now housed in the University of Knedsville-Sur-Tainly Archives, is worth the visit to the farthest outcropping in Scotland. The archivists left the notebook completely unsullied; that is to say, they left it completely sullied. We think about the folks - so-called 'preservers' of art and history - who were given the task of cleaning the ceiling of the Sistine Chapel. Um, you just don't do stuff like that.

A few readers were looking forward to the dramatic derring-do of our hero, with dazzling flashes and deep slashes from his magical blade; with stabs and jabs; with the gnashing and biting and swinging of bodies hither and thither; with blood and bones and viscera; with paper and pen scattered about willy and nilly; with last-ditch efforts; with scratching and clawing for last breaths of this sacred air before succumbing, before surrendering, before resigning to rest; the acceptance of the soil strewn with the residue of battle and bodies; the setting sun forming elongated shadows of the doomed dualists; the dread detritus, the morbid memorabilia of this superhuman conflict; and that sort of thing. Next time. We promise. Meantime, give peace a chance.

# III

*Presume Not the Carrots*

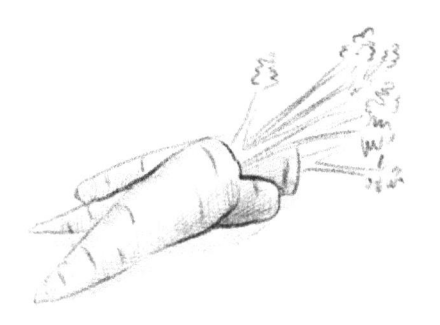

# 1

# Presume Not the Carrots (a.k.a. The Carrot Episode)

Rabbit arrived at the diner and saw Skib and the knight back in the trice. Or in the trice in the back. Or back in the trice in the back. It's all about the writing.

He waved to them and mouthed that he would be right back. Amazing what paws can do; we mean, the subtleties that can be captured and conveyed in their delicate movements. Like furry little wings on a long-eared Terpsichore, the gestures fluid as a delicate Hawaiian dance, where the hands and arms tell a story, a lovely story of the Sun befriending the Sea and their mutual affection yielding a glowing reflection for all to behold. Rabbit's story was a bit more prosaic: he had to pee before he joined them at the table.

As soon as he sat down, Tracy was there to fill his glass of water, telling him she'd be right back with his coffee and orange juice. He looked at the menu, which was a perfunctory act if there ever was one because he had it pretty much memorized, then decided on the oatmeal with fruit. Tracy was pretty good about loading lots of fruit in there: apples, bananas, blueberries, whatever was around. Before Tracy, there was a waiter named Lenny who took it upon himself to add carrots to everything Rabbit ordered, including the goddamn oatmeal. Yes, Rabbit understood, but that's stereotyping, man, and that ain't cool. Rabbit hadn't eaten carrots since his mom used to dump them in front of him about a hundred times a day when he was a kid. "It's good for your eyes," she'd say every time she served them. Every single time. Now, he'd rather eat cat fur than carrots. He couldn't help but be reminded of something he saw written on the chalkboard in front of Mel's burger joint: "Carrots may improve your vision, but alcohol will double it."

She was a good mom, though a little too doting. When she reached that age - you know the one we mean - she moved on to the greener pastures of Miami, where she chose to retire. And by greener, we mean browner, because grass doesn't stand a chance there. Rabbit calls it God's Waiting Room. God just calls it The Miami Branch of My Waiting Room. There are oodles of branches of waiting rooms. Like a billion. And that's just on this planet.

But Rabbit's Mom, Sadie, wanted to be with her friends, and that's where they were. Rabbit rarely visited because he hated sand, salt water, heat, humidity, people who clip coupons, people who pronounce "God Forbid" as "Gawd Fawbid," people who constantly kvetch, people who cover their furniture with newspapers and plastic, and people who cheat at mahjong, of all things.

So, not carrots. Tracy knew this instinctively. Don't tell anyone, but I think she's one of us.

All of this is a way of introducing what we in the business call The Carrot Episode, the *ne plus ultra* of literary vegetable segues, so let's saddle our mounts, mount our saddles, kick some hind-quarters and git a move on, as they say absolutely nowhere that is important.

The Carrot Episode begins as all such stories do, in Athens, 405 B.C., on yet another pleasant lolling afternoon in the agora down the block from Donatius of Aspergum's apartment. Donatius, the author of several plays thankfully lost in the River of

Time, was looking for ingredients for a stew. Now, this was a time and place before and to the left of the existence of the orange carrots of our time and place, so they were black or purple or blue for all I care, just not orange. You want farm talk, see Mr. Greenjeans. You want cross-breeding farm talk, see Mr. Greengenes. That's called the result of drinking and writing.

Anyway, Donatius bought his carrots, parsnip, and other ancient legumes, and strolled home. When he stepped inside his room (there was no door) there sat a god. This was not unusual; the gods would often go around to strangers' homes, sometimes disguised as common folk or even beggars, sometimes in full god garb, which was tough on the eyeballs.

In this case, it was a woman of unearthly beauty, which is a given, given the situation. Even though she wasn't at the moment giving off rays of light in every direction, you could tell this was not a woman whose feet touched the ground. Boy, was she good-looking. Being a heirophant by trade, Donatius was a tad less fazed than your average olive-weaned mook.

She was Athena. Or Aphrodite. It was a long time ago. So, this goddess is sitting in his room and it is literally impossible to get over her looks, but Donatius tries to act cool and invites her to dinner, which is the right thing to do because the Ancient Greeks believed in this thing called Xenia, which is hospitality, and they believed in it for the very reason shown here: you don't know who it really is who has come a-knockin': could be a beggar, could be a god disguised as a beggar. Best not risk offending a god, so invite her in and offer her whatever you have. Especially if she's blistering hot.

In this case, there was no question, so it was an easy decision to offer a meal. Just don't hurt me.

She gave off so much light, he didn't need a lamp to illuminate the place. She watched him rinse the vegetables in a basin and drop them in a clay thing and pour stuff in. Because she was a VIP, he even added a dash of salt, which cost a fortune in those days. And soon they were sitting at the tiny table. She barely touched her food: draw your own conclusions.

"Is the food okay?" he asked in Ancient Greek with that urban - and urbane - Athenian accent.

"Yes. You are a gracious host." (Phew.)

"Is there a reason you are here? I mean, do you wish something of me?"

She picked up a soggy something from her bowl, set it back down gingerly and said, "Yes. The Dionysian Festival is coming up in a few weeks and the play you are working on is awful. It stinks." She was right. Even if she was wrong, she was right, but she was right.

He asked, "Have you read it? Of course you have. How would you know that it stinks if you didn't read it?" He paused. "I can fix it any way you like."

"Okay, then, write this down." Donatius went to his stack of papyrus, found a workable reed, his ceramic pot of ink made from octopus juice and animal fat, and braced himself for the magic.

"First, I think I should have a bigger role. Everyone makes sacrifices to me and prays to me, but I think I should be present on stage. I'd like to be able to talk."

"Are you saying you want to be in the play? I mean, you personally want to be acting on the stage?"

"Well, it wouldn't be acting if I were playing myself, would it? And I think I'd make a good impression."

"Oh, heck yes! You'd be amazing! Dazzling! I see a winner here! But do you want me to write the words for you, or do you want to just get up there and, you know, wing it. Be yourself. Because I don't know if I could do you justice."

"Donatius, I've seen your writing and no, you could not do me justice. I'll just speak my own words, but I promise they will fit in with the rest of your play."

He was jotting madly, which was hard with a reed because each dip into the ink was good for two maybe three words before it turned into scratch.

"So," said Donatius, "you want to save the day. The whole divine intervention thing. Encourage sacrifice....more goats and bulls on the altar. Boy, you gods sure can eat. I'm doing the math. It's good PR."

"I'm doing it for the humans. I have no interest in meat." Gods are under no obligation to tell the truth, so make of her words what you will.

"Okay. For the humans. So, I'm guessing after the second antistrophe, you'll come down.....Is that it? Come down? Walk out? Suddenly appear?...."

"I'll come down. Float right onto the proscenium. Everyone on stage will take a few steps back, forming a semi-circle for me, then fall to the ground or bow or kneel. Then I'll walk to the very front and speak to the audience directly."

"Oh, the fourth-wall thing. Powerful."

"In full raiment."

"Is that legal?"

"Do you know what raiment means?"

"Sure I do. Raiment means naked."

"How can you be a playwright and a priest and not know the word, raiment? Exactly the opposite. I'll be wearing a magnificent gown. Bejeweled. Crown and all. And I shall shine like the chariot of the Sun!"

"Wow. I see trophies and purses of gold in my future!"

By now, the goddess saw that she was dealing with someone who was not Sophocles, Euripides, Aeschylus, or Aristophanes. Or even Plantarius of Fasciitis, for that matter. She decided a little inspiration couldn't hurt, so she disrobed for him, then, realizing what she had done, was obligated to turn him into a rabbit. Call it coincidence, but this rabbit was one of Rabbit's ancestors, answering the questions raised by the heretofore inexplicable DNA of our hero. Satisfied?

I want to wake up in the morning with a story to tell. (This is intended to be an allusion to a line in "Get Back" by Ludacris, not a quote, though it is a quote. It just seems to fit here.)

# 2

# A Visit to a House of Worship (It's Called Balance)

R abbit and Elephant were standing in the rear of the Cathedral of St. Peter the Enduring Rock, a Roman Catholic masterpiece. This glorious edifice stood adjacent to the Sin Won beauty supply store on Eldersend Avenue in Trespass, Nebraska. The architecture was magnificent, the building empty, save for one old man kneeling in a pew off to the side, a few feet from a plaster rendering of the seventh Station of The Cross.

The reasons for Rabbit's and Elephant's standing are obvious, given the limited capacity of the pew.

Another fellow entered, middle-aged, whatever

that is, and was walking down the right-side aisle (no symbolism intended) when he saw the old man trying to raise himself from his kneeling position. The fellow went right over to him and helped him up, then gracefully guided him to a seated position.

The old man said, "Much obliged."

"No problem, "said the other, and he began to slide out of the pew.

"Say," said the old man.

"Yessir. What can I do for you?" There wasn't the tiniest suggestion of anything but patience and kindness in this fellow's voice. When he asked, "What can I do for you?" he really meant it: it sounded as if there was nothing he would not have done for the old man.

"You're a regular."

The reply was modest: "I try to come in a couple of days a week. Clear my head. You know."

"I do."

The good Samaritan said, "Dave."

The now-seated old man said,"Lucifer."

Dave was taken aback, but he smiled at what had to be a joke. "*The* Lucifer?"

"Yes."

"Do you come here often? I don't recall seeing you here before."

"I'm here all the time."

Dave thought for a minute. "That's deep."

"You don't believe me. That's understandable. I

wouldn't, either."

Dave smiled again. "It's okay. I think as long as you're here, I suppose, you're on the right track. This is a good thing."

"Dave, you are a good person."

"Thank you. I want to say, you don't seem like such a bad guy, either, but imagine! I'm trying to figure out if that would be the biggest sin ever." Right or wrong, Dave was inclined to show respect to him, not out of fear and certainly not out of reverence, but out of appreciation—not the grateful kind—but understanding of something sacred… in the profane way. At the very least, he had been God's wing-man before what was really the Holy War.

"You believe in God?"

"I do."

"And in me?"

"I do."

"And what do I do?"

"You are the reason for the evil in the world."

"Dave, do you believe that I am the cause – the source, the reason—of the existence of cancer, plagues, earthquakes, birth defects, car accidents, murder, suicide, wars, pride, sloth, greed, wrath, lust, envy, gluttony? How about stupidity? How about negligence? Sadness, depression, loneliness. Do you believe that without me, none of these would exist? Or less of them?"

Dave was silent and Lucifer did not interfere. He

remained quiet, looking down at his hands, then up at the columns, the images of the stations of the cross, the crosses, the many crosses that filled the walls. And Mary.

Dave finally spoke again: "This is a toughy."

Lucifer said, "Let me make it even tougher. Do you believe anything can exist without God giving it the green light? Or is it just mankind, and He and I are out of the picture?"

"Out of the picture? I don't know. I have to think about this. I still believe."

"I'm not against that. I don't think it's bad at all. Especially if it makes you feel better. If it helps you get through life. Where's the harm?"

"I don't know if you're the devil or just really, really clever."

"Not much difference, really. You wouldn't believe how many clever people, smart people, there are below. We could start a tech company." He smiled. "I think we already have."

Dave was quiet again. Lucifer said, "I have to be going. It was nice meeting you, Dave." He raised himself with difficulty.

"Let me help you." He moved toward Lucifer and took his elbow, helping him navigate the narrow space. Dave moved with him slowly. When they were both in the aisle, Lucifer straightened himself up. He looked several inches taller. And younger. He stretched and grew taller still. Dave stepped back to give him room. He thought Lucifer could make himself grow enough to fill the church with himself. No need.

Dave watched the giant walk out of the church, hunching to avoid hitting his head, just missing the words appearing over the doors in mosaic, "Vade in Pace," then disappearing.

Dave put his hand on the back of the pew to hold himself up. He turned to face the front of the church, sat, then knelt, then sat, then bowed low, then looked up. Something he saw made him smile. He read the words on the wall: Sanctus Sanctus Sanctus. He took the deepest breath he ever took and spent the rest of his time wondering if this was some kind of dream or test. He sat for a long time with his head lowered and his elbows on his knees, deep, deep in thought and wondering if he should be praying instead of thinking, or if in this case, they were the same thing, or if thinking meant he had failed or passed the test. Boy, was he stuck.

Rabbit and Elephant didn't say a word as they observed this....Was it magic? This thing?

Elephant said, "Wow."

Rabbit said, "You ain't kidding."

Elephant asked, "What did that mean?"

"Beats me. I think we should ask one of the big trees back home. They know about this stuff."

They walked out, made a left and another left and were back home, where they made a left and another left and they stood before Ken The Enormous Old Oak, one of the oldest trees in the magical forest.

# 3

# An Example of Why Trees Shouldn't Be Asked Questions

**K**en listened to their story, which was remarkably like ours. He spoke: "Not far from here lived Ruben the Tree. Old, Oak, like me, but lucky. The kind of luck that defies or defines 'Meant to Be.' Centuries ago, a seed fell on an enormous flat rock, almost dead center. Being a tree, I can tell you that there are few worse places to land if you want a shot at Life. Well, sure enough, taking root was not an option, but good old Ruben, starting with the tiniest drops of water and about eight inches from anything that could pass for soil - and that was eight inches in all directions - started pushing his roots all over to feed himself. He lived to be three hundred. It was a storm that took him: a gust of wind knocked him over, and you could see that giant rock that he worked his way around. You could also see that it was because he couldn't dig down, couldn't get a good hold of the earth, that over he went. You could see it, that tangled maze of roots, and that rock that looked the same as it did before Ruben showed up. His trunk is still there; he shaved a lot of branches off his neighbors when he fell. In some ways, he's the same old tree, but a lot easier to sit on."

Elephant looked at Rabbit for some sort of sign, not knowing what to make of this story, either.

Rabbit said, "Thanks, Ken, that was some terrific babble. Wonderfully devoid of meaning or impact. You should be a writer. But could you possibly apply your many years of wisdom to answering our question?"

Ken tried again: "Very well. It's all about what things represent and what patterns are created. When you combine these two - the symbols and the patterns - you have something called meaning. You must keep in mind that symbols are open to interpretation and patterns are in the eye of the beholder. Often, we see patterns that are not there. Apophenia. Actually, Pareidolia. So, when you combine symbols that can mean many things with patterns that may or may not be there or are not what they appear, you get meaning that is at best frothy, at worst, baseless. But not useless. Not at all. Where meaning comes from and how we get it isn't relevant for it to be useful. We take the meaning because we need the meaning. We believe in it because it makes things better for us….or at least we feel that it makes things better for us, which is even better for us. Got it so far?"

"No ."

Ken continued: "Good. So, let's break your story into its key components. First, the church. You should write this down; that's how good it is. The church represents lines."

Elephant asked, "Lines?"

Ken The Tree said, "I can't work like this. Just follow me. Lines. It all comes together. It always does. It has no choice!" He was waving his branches like a tree in a tornado."

He went on: "Dave represents a sphere or ball. Lucifer, obviously, symbolizes a right triangle. The pews represent parallel lines. The aisles are perpendicular lines. You see where I'm going here?"

"No, not the slightest." It doesn't matter who said this, they both felt the same way.

"Good. The church doors represent rectangles. The kneeling another set of right triangles. The stations of the cross are the process of building a Euclidean model on a Cartesian plane. You two are two points on an oblique angle. The conversation is a multi-variable wave function using Wendley's Mass-Harbinger Function. Dave's motions are Lycoan erasures using the Lendellian Standard. See what's happening here?"

"Nope." Again, one was speaking for both.

"Excellent, we're almost there. The actress who approaches from the balcony....."

"What? There wasn't any actress! The balcony? You mean the pulpit? What......?"

"See? You missed her. And do you know why you missed her? Because you aren't trained to see what is there. But be assured, she was. And what she represents is the convergence that melds the union into a coherent orientation frame with co-linear dimensions. Imagine that she is on a trapeze made by the equilateral triangle of the Trinity, creating a co-radial relationship with humanity. Now, look at the columns through the same Mass-Harbinger Function and calculate the non-positional gaps in the partial-spherical conundrum. See? Sublime complementarity."

"Not even close," asserted Rabbit.

"It's as easy as spelling CAT. You have your C and your A and your T and get CAT. Do you see why I chose CAT and not, say, CENTRIFUGE?"

"No.'

"The C is your partial sphere, your summersault, if you will. Then your A: the symmetry, the intersections, the converging ascendants, the acute angularity. Finally, that beautiful T; the acme of perpendicularity, of balance, of symmetry, and the rood. It's practically the same story all over again, but told in three letters! How could it be any simpler?"

There was a brief period of sighing, head shaking, the odd moan, the monad (which is the odd moan inverted), the shuffling of feet great and small. the sense that time has greater value than we attribute to it, then Elephant spoke. "The story is all arithmetic?"

Ken The Tree was relieved. "Yes. You see, sir, it's a geometric universe. A clockwork universe, if you will. The universe - even the soul - is a matter of mathematics, physics, I dare say, logic. You understand completely."

Rabbit looked at Elephant and said, "Really?"

Elephant was beaming. "I got it right.'

"Got what right? This is all banana oil."

Elephant used a voice he never used before: the pedant: 'That's because you didn't understand it."

"No, William F. Buckley, it's because it was nonsense."

"Mr. Tree..."

"Ken, please."

"Ken, what do you do when you have someone who just doesn't get it? Who can't see what is right in front of them?' This was Elephant, who for just this moment had borrowed Ken The Tree's sense of irrefutability.

In anticipation of the answer, Rabbit wished he were sitting on the stool next to Augustine.

*Et factum est.*

# 4

# And We Come Full Circle

E lephant found his friend being gamely supported by the bar and ignored by Augustine the wolf, who had grown tired of Rabbit's diatribe about Ken The Tree's exegesis, which according to Rabbit could only be justified by the conflation of too much education and too much Papaver somniferum certainly absorbed through the roots. He walked in just as Rabbit was using his favorite inebriated transitional phrase: "And another thing."

"…And another thing. Wait, what was I just saying? Oh, yeah, and another thing, you look at all this stuff (he did a one-paw wave because the other was busy keeping his head from landing on the bar) and you say, 'oh, look a square! And over there, those mountains, those are triangles. And this planet, a sphere. And this road here, that's a squiggly line!' You see what I mean?"

Ironically, Augustine was in the same mood Rabbit was in an hour ago; that is to say, wishing he were somewhere else so he wouldn't have to hear a bunch of baloney. That's called the Circle of Life. It's from a very good movie. Very good!

The funny part is that Ken The Tree was right. Not as right as, say, Benjamin The Redwood, who had about a thousand years of knowledge under his trunk, but right is right. There is, for example, this entity called the Cosmic Bubble – when God pronounces it, the 'S' is silent – more commonly called The Local Bubble. You know what's located in the Local Bubble? Earth, our solar system, our galaxy and all the galaxies in our neighborhood. What makes sense is that this Bubble is in a part of space that's even emptier than normal space: an emptier vacuum! Less than nothing! You want meaning? Consider the fact that we all exist in the emptiest part of the universe. The void that other voids aspire to be. We literally live in less than nothing. No wonder we have to make up everything: there is only so much nothing we critters can take.

Augustine didn't even look at Elephant, who was now standing right behind his slumping friend; the barkeep said, "Mr. Bunny here is two sheets to the wind. Take him home, and if not home, anywhere that is not the bar."

# 5

# And We're Back

Elephant felt a bit guilty: he had never been smart before - that is to say, he never felt smart before; not that he felt stupid, just not smart - and the feeling went right to his vocal cords, unbeknownst to him until he heard his own voice. He believed this is what drove Rabbit to the bar. It wasn't, but misunderstandings like this are abundant in both worlds.

He gently wound his trunk around his buddy who made no objection, and allowed himself to be carried out.

The night was exactly as it was painted to be. That's a tautology, but it's meant to convey something. Let's move on.

The night was exactly as it should have been on a clear, cool night far from the city. Cities are not good for nights, unless you want a painting of night in a city. But here we want the big picture without high-rises punching holes in it. Like a spectacular butterfly impaled on a pin: those magical wings belied by, given the lie by a simple pin. This may be a commentary on the frailty of life or Life. We won't keep doing this uppercase-lowercase thing. It's the small thing annihilating the big thing, but not in the David versus Goliath way, in the way a mosquito causes a plague or a bomb turns a museum into dust or Camus dying in a car accident or a French Symbolist Poet hanging himself in an alleyway. The point is, Rabbit needed unobstructed, untainted night. Though this is an antidote for *weltschmertz*, it doesn't do much for besotted rabbits. Being a spiritual whooshponder, Elephant held Rabbit up to the stars, hoping to purge him of the booze-and-drug bug. Depending on your definition of vomiting, you could say it worked, which did nothing for Elephant's sinuses.

# IV

*Why Not?*

**Rabbit and Elephant wanted to take a shot at acting. No kidding. Here's how it started:**

# 1

# Acting: A Play

Our heroes were sitting in front of a pond and watching the wildlife do its thing.

Elephant sighed and said, "Sometimes we go and sometimes we stay."

Rabbit thought this was actually a good start for something, so he said, "Keep going."

"We go or we stay, but I'm always a Whooshponder and you're always a rabbit."

"Not *a* rabbit! *The* Rabbit. Rabbit! Have you been following our story?"

"I mean we're the same. We don't become things we are not, no matter where we go."

"Is that good or bad?"

"As you would say: Precisely! I don't know. Maybe we should be other creatures. Maybe that would be fun."

"Would you want to be Rabbit?"

"Yes, yes I would. I would like to know what that's like. Would you like to be me?"

Trapped! Rabbit could not say, "No, no way, not in a million years, Never." That would be wrong. He had to come up with an answer that wouldn't hurt his friend. So, he said, "You bet."

"I have a great idea! Let's become actors. We can learn to be each other....or anyone else we want to be! What's better: same creatures, different places or different creatures, same places?"

"That's pretty good. You know what? I'm in. Let's try different!" thereby clarifying nothing.

"Elephant asked another good question; "Is that why creatures become actors? To be different? To be not-themselves? And why? Do they not like themselves? Maybe they just want attention? Or maybe they're like us and just want to see what it's like to be other creatures."

"I know a place where we can get the answers and learn to act. Are you busy right now?" (That was humor.) "Follow me. And you know what's great? Our mission will start to be fulfilled right away: we'll learn what it's like to be other creatures, namely actors! And sometimes you can learn about yourself just by putting yourself in other creatures' psyches; when you figure them out, you figure yourself out. I, sir, am a genius!";

"Me, too! Me, too!" said Elephant, and they were off.

There was an acting studio close by (duh) and they were able to join a class of fellow aspiring thespians, and some Rabbit and Elephant knew, so there were plenty of waves and nods and shaking of hands before things got rolling.

The teacher was none other than Rita Lovedrench, blur of stage and screen, Academy Award usher, Tony Award deliverer, Lidley Spillage Award winner for her supporting role as the supporting parent in Suppurating Conniptions, directed by Parly Truce. She retired in 1940, when she did not get the role of her dreams, sixteen-year-old Kindy Ford, in "Kindy, Go Home". Rita was sixty-six at the time. She then opened her acting school on 10th Avenue, in her living room.

She was a terrific teacher, as scores of her students who made it all the way to auditions will attest. Rita welcomed her new students with open arms, and gave them the two second tour: the stage was a rug in the middle of the stage….um….living room; there were fewer than ten chairs of all types around it. Her classes were a delightfully mixed bag: humans, animals, creatures of all kinds. Everyone got along, the mood of the classes was simultaneously light and serious.

The key to becoming an actor is to act. So: find

the character and learn the lines, or find the character by learning the lines, or understand the lines by understanding the character: so they would read and analyze and speak the lines. Avoid overacting. You cannot be too subtle.

Let's take a peek.

### Act III, Scene iv

(Aurelia and Pushkin's Villa in L'Aredo, late afternoon on the veranda overlooking MacSorkin's Poodle. Both lie on their lounge chairs and through their teeth. And, yes, it's lie, not lay.)

Aurelia is played by Chase Windlass of Deep Spasm, New Jersey. Pushkin is played by Elephant. Their quiet will be disrupted by the appearance of Jesstome Fordasummer, played by Ellen The Earthworm, who has had acting aspirations since she was knee-high to a grain of sand, and, despite her speech impediment, she has been told she's a natural. The other voice will be Rita's, either when she is reading stage directions or making the odd suggestion or correction.

Aurelia (puffing on her topiary): I'm angry.
Pushkin: I, too, am angry. In fact, I am furry us.
Rita: Furious.

Pushkin. Oh. In fact, I am furious.

Rita: A little more emotion. Remember, Pushkin has just been told that he does not exist.

Aurelia: Yes, this is quite the inconvenience.

(Enter Jesstome Fordasummer in a wet-suit): A-ha! Ha hav fhah nedu!

Rita: Now try to enunciate a little better.

Jess: A-ha! Hi Haf fhound dew!

Rita: Better. One more time.

Jess: A-ha! I have found you!

Rita: Good. Continue.

Aurelia: Jess! How is the fondue?

Rita: What?

Aurelia: Just kidding. How did you find me?

Jess: I searched high and low, I followed the map of my heart, listened to the music of the mountains, followed the vibrations beneath my feet, let my love move the sails that would bring me to you! Be mine, Aurelia, as you were meant to be

Aurelia: hmmmmmm.....Perhaps I shall. Now that we have found out that Pushkin does not exist, I may be available.

Rita: Excellent! Bravo! Brava! Let's take a little breather and talk a bit. Ellen, you have wonderful stage presence.

Ellen blushed at the compliment and Elephant felt a bit jealous. Chase joined the French Foreign Legion.

Rita: "Ellen, tell us how you tapped into your character."

Ellen mulled for a moment. "I feel like I've been there. I know what Jess has been through. I've searched and searched for....for that special someone... (she choked up a bit, then pulled herself together)... looking without having a way. Without knowing how or where to look. It would seem like wandering, aimless wandering, but something was moving me. Something was causing me to choose one direction over another. But it takes me. Funny, I suppose something has to move you... forward, I mean." She became lost in thought.

"Excellent. That's a lesson for all aspiring actors. The character can have something that you can connect to. Look carefully. It isn't always obvious. Look deeply. Ellen found it right away, but it can take a long time. Good." She turned to Elephant. "Elephant, tell us about Pushkin."

Elephant was as nervous about this as he had been about reading his lines, so while Ellen was speaking, he was planning his answer. "He's angry. No, he's furious."

"Good. Good start. And why is he furious?"

"He found out that he doesn't exist. So, he's pretty upset."

"Yes," said Rita, "Now, why would that be? Let's dig down a bit."

Elephant thought. Ellen crocheted. Rabbit banged his head against the wall. Chase felt the bracing salt air on his face as the ship sailed him to Europe. Rita considered that job at the carnival.

Coincidentally, just as Chase was disembarking in London where he would stay with a friend for a few days before crossing the channel to France, Elephant had his answer. He began cautiously, tentatively, as if his answer to the question why a person would be upset when he discovered he did not exist were important. And then there's the whole paradox thing: if you don't exist, being upset about it seems a tad unlikely. And who, precisely, was the person who apprised him of his non-existence, and how did that come about? The "Hello, you don't exist" approach is tough to swallow since it would result in the classic subway parry: "Then why are you talking to me?"

Elephant said, "Because if he doesn't exist, he spent too much money for that nice house. He could have gone way cheaper."

Rita searched for the words, then said, "Yes, what you are saying is that Pushkin has invested too much in a life that wasn't. He realizes the futility of all he has done. He is not even a shadow of a shadow. And worst of all, he must be wondering, 'Now that I know this terrible thing, what do I do next? What can I do next?' What a terrible spot poor Pushkin is in. Good work."

Elephant added triumphantly, "That's like a lot of creatures. Especially the ones not from around here." Rabbit stopped banging his head to look at his friend who had suddenly turned into Soren Kierkegaard.

Ellen The Earthworm was smitten. The lesson here is that if you want to woo any member of the phylum Annelida, talk like a philosopher. They are suckers for that kind of stuff. It goes back to their early history, which, unlike certain species, did not allow their accomplishments, from the literary to the scientific to the architectural, to disappear from their sphere. They were natural archeologists; their digging was their way of getting from one floor to the next in the great living museum that is history and contemporaneity. Imagine if your species was able to let your past, present and future coexist without the sacrifice of one for the other. Imagine a human taking a walk from one century to another, from Ancient Greece to the middle ages to the Industrial Age in one beautifully damp, cool, overcast day? Not that the weather matters: their world is all underfoot, woven among living and dead roots.

The earthworm society has a wormhole - in fact, that's where the term comes from; worms' spatial-temporal tunnels. This was applied ironically and optimistically to the theoretical wormholes of the human astrophysicists - again - theorizing the existence of something that already exists and that is being utilized in the most productive ways. Sure, earthworms are more intelligent than humans, but also - or perhaps because so- they have a greater respect for civilizations, no matter whose.

The reason the above paragraph appears is not only to teach a bit of history; not only to act as a segue from the prior paragraph; but to be the transition to our next consideration: namely, humans suck.

# 2

# A Little Etymology

The word "Human comes from Kybberian-Caulto, the language of a conflation of nomadic tribes who crapped all over north-eastern Europe before it was Europe and north-eastern of anywhere. They were known for their inexplicable, unpredictable violence. A now classic example comes from Wynt's *Historium*, which describes a battle between the Kybberians and another nomadic horde, the Shmaggegs or Shmaggegies. As the two armies faced each other, the Kybberians suddenly turned on each other, slashing and stabbing and clubbing each other as the Shmaggegs watched, dumbfounded. Was this, perhaps, some tactic to lure them in or to unsettle them? Or for them to assume that the Kybberians had been turned into indiscriminatingly bloodthirsty animals who could never be defeated? Some of the Shmaggegs urged retreat; others, the opposite: a storm of arrows and a quick attack. But the elder soldiers showed their wisdom by telling them to stand and watch. So, they did, until they sat and watched, then reclined and watched from their positions the self-annihilation of their enemies, blessing the obvious intervention of their gods. Within an hour, there was no army left for the Shmaggegs to battle.

A bloody, bloodless victory.

Anyway, they used the word "human," pronounced "Qmnmnnnmn" with every letter clearly enunciated, to mean "a ladder without rungs." Hence, their word for something so useless that it isn't merely unrecognizable as something that simply doesn't work, but as something so useless it cannot be recognized as being unrecognizable. Hence, Human.

That takes us to this:

# 3

# Man and Nature

As history shows, Man is the only creature who works hard to claim to care about other creatures: save the whale; save the rainforest; save the wolf; and so on ad nauseum. At the same time, He obliterates all of them without batting an eye. Okay, then.

When Man renders himself extinct, do you think the animals will shed a tear? More likely the rhinos, leopards, elephants, bees, butterflies, not to mention the trees and flowers and rivers will be dancing and singing and shouting for joy at the demise of the toxic vermin that is Man. Yes, there will be a period of scorched-earth recovery, but eventually the grass will take hold again and the planet will flourish. And this time, when god does the Adam and Eve thing again. Eden will kick their asses, and introduce them to that little pool of quicksand behind those bushes over there. When was the last time Nature had spring in its step? I mean outside of the magical forest?

Humans. And yet. And yet.

# 4

# Enough Rhetoric! Let's Get Deep!

E lephant, Rabbit and Drake the Swan (yes, the irony is not lost on us) were carefully examining the bit of nature that presented itself to them. This scrutiny was a meditative trick: one would find an image - choose an image - and look at it with the intention of seeing it. One would study it, attempt to distinguish every detail, every change in color or shade, height or depth, smoothness or roughness, the tiniest motion... and note it. The goal of this meditation was to take one out of oneself so one can purge oneself, so one can see oneself anew. You would see the new self as a part of the image before one. And if we use the word 'one' one more time in this passage one will be taken to the woodshed. Shin-Su is the philosopher who first taught this technique back in Long Island City, New York, circa last week.

There they sat. Elephant said—and he was probably speaking for all— "My butt is falling asleep." And by "butt," he meant "brain."

# 5

# Snakes

Snakes are interesting. They're smart and their impact on mankind is inestimable. Consider our comrade in the garden of Eden. Ponder our pal in the story of Gilgamesh. Contemplate our confederate in the *Tale of Tyrentius*. Try to fathom our fellow in Bellerphon's *Eudaiyaton*. Agonize over our amigo Nidhogg in the Norse sagas. Visualize Veles and Volos. Query Quetzacoatl. You're talking some powerful mojo. Think Cthonic. Then check for a thpeech impediment.

But are there snake-holes? No. Well, yes, but not in the sense of wormholes. The fact that you have to —at best—hyphenate snake-holes tells you that holes are not what snakes are known for. A snake hole sounds unworthy of a snake. We're talking real snakes not human snakes: a snake hole for a human snake is completely apropos.

Snakes are about the present. Their interaction with the overwhelming "Now" certainly paradoxically resonates throughout time, but nonetheless they are focused on that one point that is most potent and most transient. Try measuring it. Worms, as we noted, are all over the place when it comes to time. It's a different kind of smart. Perhaps the difference between Knowledge and Intelligence, modulo morals, ethics, history as foundation versus history as malignancy, growth versus decay, Truth versus deception, disguise, facade, ruse, disingenuousness… e.g."all progress is good" "new is better than old" "don't look back, look forward" "Excelsior!" "Fast is better than slow". And don't call an earthworm a hypocrite when she reminds us that the early worm catches the dirt. They don't exclude the present; they simply put it in context.

Earthworms believe in the simultaneity of all times. Believe? No! They know the simultaneity of all times: their hallways and corridors and passageways will take them seamlessly through this simultaneous existence. Are there chambers on every level that have grown dim, are less visited, sometimes even ignored? Yes. Are some more popular than others?

Yes. Earthworms enjoy comparing and debating the merits of these rooms: the sages among them rue their own lack of time to take in all that time offers. It is the very old and the very young that dig the deepest, the former for knowledge, the latter for adventure. Some young ones have something called curiosity, an odd striving for what is not immediately visible; so much so, that they are willing to exert themselves to see what is beyond and what is beyond still.

Snakes know the truth of temporal simultaneity, too, but they don't want anyone else to know; it's harder to move creatures around when they have those deep roots. Manipulation requires shallowness and ignorance. Boy, do snakes love stupid.

# 6

# Music is Awesome

Elephant and Rabbit were getting a little tour from Ellen the Earthworm underground. And if you're going to fixate on how Elephant negotiated the corridors of that time-space, we're not going to get anywhere, least of all, to Vienna in 1783 to visit Wolfgang Amadeus Mozart in the apartment of his friend Ernst Fingtlizen, at 5 Zauberflotestrasse Nibelungentindorfen, on the second floor overlooking the Verklartenachtessgarten Rosenkavalierenshoen Zimfernest in Aufshalder-Dundervloss across from the monument to Hammerklavier Mittgershovellstetzenfleitt. And you should know better.

We don't know if you've ever heard ol' Mozart playing violin, but it's quite the treat. He was even better on the ol' 88's, which back then was the ol' 60's because he played the pianoforte, which was shorter, ebonies and all, so we're talking about five octaves, but his real strength was putting little ovals - some filled in, some left empty - on groups of five horizontal lines - some with flags, some upside-down, that, when translated by humans for the express purpose of interacting with oddly-shaped bits of wood and wire and metal wound all around each other, create miracles.

Elephant had never seen marks like these and for the life of him he could not figure out how one oval in one place meant one sound and a lopsided wheel in a different place, another sound. He saw what Mozart was doing; studying those shapes in those positions and at the same time doing another strange thing; pushing and pulling... was it a length of wood? A ribbon? A wire?... across other wires on... Oh! it was just too much that was foreign to him. And the sound was impossible! Coming from that little bit of wood sitting on the fellow's shoulder and held firmly by his chin, came... for crying out loud... music.

Elephant was enthralled. "What is that?" he whispered.

Rabbit whispered back, "That's music."

"But I've heard music. All kinds…"

Wofgang was working the bow in long, slow strokes, envisioning the music that Anton Stabler would play on the clarinet; in other words, unusually high notes, like for the Clarinet Quintet or the Clarinet Concerto. Elephant started tearing up, not because the music was sad, but because it was supernal. Creatures who walk around on this, our little sphere, simply cannot make sounds like this, he thought.

Rabbit said, "What's wrong?"

"I don't know. I'm not sad. But the music is...."

"Yep. This guy can really mess with your head. Happy, sad, lonely, angry.'

'Does he have a different box for each one?'

"Nope. Same box. Watch." He turned to Mozart and said, "Give him a little something to lighten his mood." Mozart changed his tune; Elephant was practically dancing, which means he was swaying and swinging tail and trunk, knowing better than to do the old foot-stomping thing he does when he's doing his version of floating on air, which is exactly the opposite of floating on air. If some poet came up with a metaphor for floating on air (go on: tell us that's already a metaphor) like this: "he was so happy, his mass displaced volumes of terrestrial matter regardless of density when said mass was applied to targeted locations by the intended motion of said mass meeting said terrestrial matter or mass of constituent elements of lesser density than the mass that would impact it." If that doesn't make you all tingly inside, you are an antiquated cyclotron. Like a bolo.

We thought we were finished, but our bow is merely suspended above the strings; our hands merely pausing above the keys. (Get it? Keys? Piano keys or keys to the door of revelation. We're killin' it, here.) Sometimes, words are attached to music. Sometimes, this is another level of paradise, like when the words are poetry in and of themselves: by definition, beautiful and True. Some would say those two qualities are one and the same, but there is an ugly truth, lots of them, in fact, so I respectfully disagree, Plato. But he would say, the mere fact that it is true makes it beautiful, whether it's a pianoforte dropped on our cat or not. Your cat: I don't own a cat.

Music doesn't lie. M. C. Kleinvelt says that this is because it comes from heaven. He's the guy who cuts my hair, but back in the old country he was a beautician.

Whitman was wrong, as usual. I mean Walt. He heard music in everything: way to aim low. Sounds are not necessarily music; sounds can lie: for example, the banging of a hammer on steel can be oppression disguised as liberty; the banging of a senator on a lectern, same thing. Poets are supposed to know this stuff.

Sometimes, humans try to be tricky and they attach untrue words to true music in an attempt to make us think the words are as true as the music. Just a little caveat. Humans do this all the time, attaching pretty things to ugly things to try to persuade you that the ugly things aren't ugly. We'll return to this later.

# 7

# Finishing the Tour Thing

Ellen loved this stuff. Giving the tour, seeing the expressions on the critters' faces. Yes, it was like showing off, but that was only part of the pleasure.

They thanked Mozart effusively, then headed out.

As they walked down the hallway, passing the numberless doors and stairwells and the plain old holes in the floor, walls and ceiling, Ellen stopped and said, "Check this out."

The door was difficult to open because of the foliage that blocked it from top to bottom. They pushed it a bit, then squeezed themselves in. Or out.

First of all, it was hot and very green.

Elephant said, "I know this place.'

Ellen said, "Wait a sec."

In a moment, a little whooshponder skipped by, followed by its mother, who was out of breath keeping up with her little son.

'That's me! That's me! And my mother! We're in the past!"

Ellen wanted to explain the Mozart visit to him, but let it go."

Rabbit couldn't: "This is all in the past. Distant past, recent past, but all past."

Elephant wasn't listening; he was enraptured watching his childhood self frolic.

"Can I say hello?"

"Not a good idea. Let's watch a bit more, then we'll go."

Elephant was too grateful to object, but did ask if they could visit again.

Ellen smiled. "As long as we can push that door open, yes."

Boy, it's going to be great getting back to the diner.

# 8

# A Prelude to Something

When it came to relatives, few creatures could boast more than Rabbit. His kind are renowned for their knack for procreation. We mention this because some of his relatives are rather well known, even popular, in circles larger than that of the magical forest, as large as that may be. Cousins named Peter, Harvey, Crusader, Jessica and Roger, Velveteen, Ricochet, Oswald, Flopsy, and Thumper among many others. Then you've got your so-called 'bunnies': Easter, Hefner's, Bugs, and oodles more, and they all have teams of lawyers, whom we anticipate hearing from before you turn the page. We have to tread carefully here because we are going to be discussing rabbit royalty, creatures of great stature, icons, celebrities, treasures of their breed, perfectly created by their perfect creator, so much so that we are humbled, hence, again, cautious in our handling of this next episode. In deference to these idols, Skib will be writing with a quill on parchment. Elephant will hold above him an oil lamp to provide the critical illumination from overhead to create the atmosphere of the faithful monk lucubrating in the scriptorium, silent save for the scratching of his reed. Our oratory may seem overblown, but presently you will be nodding your head in affirmation and approbation and will be aflutter when you meet our next guests. The only creature who is not impressed by these literary constellations is Rabbit, but they are his kin, and though we will see them in a salutary light, he will see them as cousin so-and-so and other cousin so-and-so. And so…

# 9

# We Don't Know: We Haven't Written This Yet

Rabbit, Elephant and Skib took the path to a part of the forest that Skib and Elephant were unfamiliar with. Correction: that part of the forest that was unfamiliar to Skib and Elephant. Our apologies to Mr. McCartney, our sixth-grade English teacher.

It was darker, deeper, damper, denser—are any of these words? We are trying to be alliterative, but what are we sacrificing? Denser? Actually, we're trying to build up suspense; the alliteration is on the house, but you can hose it off if you don't wait too long.

This part of the forest was somehow manicured, the grass cut, the flowers deliberately planted in patches and along paths, trees and hedges in good order. It was summer-like, a drowsy day here; Skib and Elephant felt sleepy; Rabbit knew better: "'Dull reality,' my foot," he thought. He looked around, sensing his cousin would pop in at any moment. And he did.

First, he looked nothing like Rabbit except that he was a rabbit. But he was white and had pink eyes…and, of course, a waistcoat and a pocket-watch and a British accent and said, "Oh, dear! Oh, dear!" incessantly. Rabbit rolled his eyes at his cousin's chronic agitation. "Nigel, calm down for two seconds, will you? You're not going to miss anything, except possibly every fashion trend since the Civil War. Tell us that's the wrong continent; we know it's the wrong continent, but the time is the time. Actually, that's not true, either: the times could not have been more different: America at the end of the Civil War and Victoria's and Dickens' England. This really puts a crimp on the relevance of Time. *A Crimp in Time*: now if that isn't the name of a book waiting to happen, we don't know what is. And don't tell us a crimp is a wrinkle; that just shows a lack of nuance.

What the two ends of the rabbit hole have in common is their disrespect, disregard, disdain, and cluelessness about Time. In the case of Rabbit's cousin, known by the sobriquet The Mad Hatter, Time had to be terminated with extreme prejudice; and so he did. By doing so, Time ended in that part of the world, defenestrated if you will.

When the Mad Hatter murders Time, it ceases, to be unnecessarily obvious.

Elephant asked, "If he murdered Time, what do we move through?"

Rabbit answered, "Pages."

"Oh."

After a rather cool exchange between the cousins, more like diplomats than relatives, the four of them sat down to tea and profundity or as a certain author would say it, profunditea. Huzzah for the apropos portmanteau!

"We have a saying down here: 'Looks like you've fallen up the rabbit hole.' That world up there," he pointed overhead, "is obviously allergic to reason. To logic. Those creatures put things on paper that are beautiful, but they don't seem to understand what they have written. Declarations and manifestos and speeches and sermons: sensible sounds translated into rubbish: no, the other way. Listen to the leaves on a windy day and you will hear sensible sounds, too, but less prone to stupidity. We have another saying: Before they are stripped into parchment, trees convey a greater truth."

Many people ask, "Can we get a little glimpse of the other end of the rabbit hole?" We hand them our binoculars.

# V

## The other side of Rabbit Hole

# Elephant and Rabbit and Didi and Gogo

Elephant and Rabbit were walking down what at least one playwright referred to as a 'country road' when they came across two characters who were the paragon of the tragicomic downtrodden. The epitomes of the downcast. The exemplars of the grim, despairing, hopeless, discarded, bereft human. If you poured a barrel of good luck on their heads, not a drop would stick to them. It would pool at their feet and drain into the soil leaving not a trace. The aforementioned unmentioned playwright might label them 'disjecta."

These two fellows were seated on the ground. They wore bowler hats and what had once been suits. They were barefoot except for the one sock that one of them wore. Their shoes – the color is open for debate – lay beside them. Behind them was a tree that – yes, this will sound absurd – they must have brought with them because it seemed out of place despite being surrounded by magical forest. In this case, the emphasis is on forest.

Rabbit and Elephant approached them. Introductions were made: Rabbit, Elephant, Didi, Gogo.

And the tree, named Rood. She explained their lot:

"You are right. This is not my domain. These gentlemen suffer from a common ailment, called 'All Too Human.' It is a condition so severe and debilitating that they cannot see any other tree but me. They cannot see the pond, the brooks, those places that offer shade, that offer respite. They are gasping for air when it is plentiful. They either crawl or they are immobile. They consider themselves magicians because they can feign their own existence. There is a poet who wrote about a man who asserted his own existence and the universe's retort to the man's vehemence."

Gogo overheard this and said, "I know how the universe feels. It's a big club. I've felt it." He rubbed the top of his head indicating precisely where he felt it. "Didi and I have tried everything to make the universe take us seriously. Or at least to acknowledge us. Just a nod would do. Our appetites are small. Am

I right, Didi? So little. Shoes that don't hurt our feet. A radish or two. But."

Didi turned to Gogo: "This is an odd pair: a bunny and a pachyderm."

"We have met stranger pairs."

"Good point. It makes me think of those people... and mirrors. Dastardly things, mirrors!"

Elephant asked, "Can't you see where you are? Just ask. This place is for everyone."

Gogo said, "Charity! No, sir. We are proud men. We are who we are. We defy...." He shook his fist at the sky. No offense was taken.

Rood said, "Their fate is their own doing. Their state is self-made. They cling to what they are and what they have. Noble men of straw."

" But even here?" Rabbit asked.

"Especially here. Their blindness is spectacular. Their self-torment, incomparable... except for all those other humans. How can they appreciate this place when they can't see it or smell it or hear it or feel it or taste it? Only the rarest of their kind - some are called poets - escape this fate. But Fate has little tolerance for creatures who fly by those nets. Fate insists on having the last word. Luckily, she has not found this place. Or perhaps she merely allows, even in her universe, a little refuge."

Rabbit knew that trees could be profound; they literally connected earth and sky; their roots at one end, their leaves at the other, always moving and growing and, most importantly, receiving. Trees are always embracing. They take in everything. But this tree had been around. He had a deep respect for such a bastion of not just knowledge, but wisdom. In mathematical form: knowledge + pain = wisdom.

Didi said, "It's time to go."

Gogo looked at his wrist where once upon a time there had been a watch and said, "I agree."

Elephant asked why. "Because," Gogo explained, "It's always time. Always. You can almost hear it."

So, up they stood – a Herculean effort – and almost forgetting their shoes, but only almost – they hobbled down the road. Their road. Rood turned to Elephant and Rabbit and wished them well, darn near bowed, and rose to follow the two orphans, looking more like a cloud than a tree.

As they faded down their path, Elephant asked, "That's a strange name. Rood. What does it mean?"

Rabbit explained, "It's like a lot of words; it has more than one meaning. One of them is a measurement of about twenty-four inches."

"Oh, so about a quarter of a centipede. He seemed bigger than that."

"It's all relative, my friend."

As they walked, Gogo felt something on his wrist. It was a watch. He was astounded: "I lost this…I thought I lost this years ago. My watch! Where….? How…?" As we can all guess, the watch was a gift from the magical forest. Alas, on the wrist of the likes of this soul, perhaps it was more a curse than a blessing: the omnipresent tick-tock of Time and the obligatory pretense of our control of it.

Didi said, "This changes everything."

Gogo replied, "We could trade it in for new socks."

"Imagine! New socks! Things are finally turning around."

"Or we could keep the watch and always know what time it is."

"I don't know which matters more."

"Excellent point. Perhaps we shouldn't rush into anything."

"A wise decision."

# VI

## The return from The Rabbit Hole

# 1

# The Return from The Rabbit Hole

**with relief and gratitude to those responsible**

Wherein the baton is handed back to Skib Bricluster, and by baton, we mean pen. You can't write with a baton, unless it's in the sand, but since one of our themes is the immortality of the written word, sand is not the best medium, though sand does beat air. Actually, that is not one of our themes, but it should be; all of the great writers were big on this: how language outlasts all that temporal, mortal, transitory, ephemeral, fleeting stuff. So, we're going to have to find a way, like maybe words carved into a tree; or a letter in a bottle; or words etched into the base of what once was an enormous statue of a king found in the sands of desert, surrounded for miles and miles by nothing. So, in order of durability from least to most, we have arrogant and/or naïve humans, their supposed enduring mighty works, the work of the sculptor, the words of the poet, but not the poet; the poet is in the first category, being insanely impermanent, wildly transitory, unusually short-lived, almost as if, having writ, moves on.

Yes, words are body, blood, mind, spirit and soul, but they are not substitutes for the taste of an apple, the sound of a piano, the sight of an ocean, the feel of the wind, the smell of fresh pizza from a New York City pizzeria. Yet, without these ridiculous scratches and scrawls and marks, what are we? What do we do? What lasts? What remains?

Even the statue, the mightiest statue, becomes a mystery, a masterpiece connected to nothing, related to nothing, a paean to emptiness, to pointless existence. Even Shelley said, without the poet, a rock is just a rock. Same with a carved rock. Rocks know this. They aren't stupid; they're just silent. They should be the very things we aspire to be: time transcendent and utterly at peace. They are completely connected to the planet and the universe. Under natural circumstances, they are impervious yet receptive. When humans get their paws on them, they are changed every which way, but their *ousia*—their essence—remains.

Thus spoke the squirrel. Sitting on the branch of a tree, her view obstructed only when a breeze comes and moves the leaves in gentle waves of air, she wonders if, when her vision is thus momentarily blocked, she has the right to assume that she knows what is happening below, or if she should be honest and write "view hampered for two seconds. Can I assume? Should I assume? Alas! How great and how small my burden to record this history!"

# 2

# A Note

This is a note that was found in a bottle that once held a coquettish little sauvignon blanc, but was now destined for other purposes. It washed up on the banks of the river that ran through the magical forest. It had traveled 5,887 nautical miles, much of it back and forth, but if you include the ups and downs, it actually traveled 7,723 nautical miles. The sea rolls, sometimes like a hamster wheel, or churns, if you prefer your seas less predictable and more volatile. It began its journey... no, it began its mission... no, not right, either... it was selected... damn it... it was found on a beach by a middle-aged goat-herd named Kelltfram Theodcyng, who was remembering his recently-departed wife by drenching himself in the spray and surf of the ocean as indifferent to Man's suffering as any deity Man had created. From his cottage, it was a short walk to the desolate strand, first through the tall grass, then the descent, then the level beach itself.

The note read:

Friend - Sometimes, the grail is the dragon, the dragon the grail. Not the gaining of a chalice, but the battle for it. After the battle, when the combatants sit, bleeding, battered, exhausted, and – yes – half-smiling, is the fleeting moment of bliss. Of serenity. The moment will disappear and will be recalled months and years and centuries later in the minds of the contestants and in the words of the bards. I shall soon be gone. I leave these words to you: the dragon is not your enemy.
*Deo Volente.*
Sir Linus Palleinsus.
*Vade in Pace.*

Kelltfram took the note and carefully placed it back in the bottle and recapped it. He didn't know what to do with it: keep it, return it to the sea with a looping toss, or drop it and let nature decide if its journey should be recommenced.

Kelltfram was Skib Bricluster's great-grandfather. Skib had heard the story from his grandfather and from his father. Of course, his first question after the first telling was, "What did he do?" Skib was twelve when he was first told this tale.

His grandfather's answer: "He never said. Even the day it happened. He – your great-grandfather – sat down at the table with us – my mother, my brothers and sisters – and we asked the same question: "What did you do? What did you do?"

"My children, I cannot say. I believe... I believe... I'm not supposed to say. I don't know why. I believe perhaps it's between me and Sir Linus, or me and the ocean... or just me. Just me."

It's funny how quickly a story can change just from the entrance of one character. Everything: the plot, the mood, the other characters....

That, dear friend, is for another day. The rising sun erases the stars. The knight sits at the counter in the diner. Elephant and Rabbit will soon arrive. The universe will be happy.

# 3

# One for the Road

It was late into a dreary night – yes, even the magical forest has times like these - the kind that causes introspection and rumination, stirring shadows and summoning spirits, glimmerings and gloom, art and alliteration…. you know the drill, when Rabbit and Elephant were visited by a raven. No, not a raven: The Raven. There are not many celebrities around these parts, but The Raven, capital T, capital R, definite article because he's the definite article, is one. He's actually been to the "Night's Plutonian shore." We're talking Styx, here. Or Phlegethon, Cocytus, Lethe, or Acheron. Anyway, the rivers of Hades. They're all pretty bleak; we're not talking beach blankets and sunscreen, here. But let's stick with Styx.

Elephant never saw Rabbit show—and we mean like he was wearing it on his sleeve—so much respect or awe; he was almost nervous. Remember: in the magical forest, Rabbit is the rock, he is the personification of Reason and Fortitude and Patience, but inexplicably with cute little bunny ears, but when The Raven landed before them.... Were those beads of sweat on Rabbit's little forehead? All Elephant saw was a very black bird, the kind of black that denies – or affirms - the existence of light, which makes sense given that he came from a place where even fire gives no light. Ask Job. Ask Milton. If Elephant knew what personification was, he would have said this bird was Hell personified.

The Raven stood on a round stone and smiled. "Reminds me of a certain bust above a chamber door. Ah, good times."

"Why did you say all that stuff? All that Lenore stuff?"

"I didn't say a word. Or rather, I only said a word. People's imaginations will take them to all kinds of dark places. Imagine: one word and the fellow calls me 'bird or fiend' and 'bird or devil.'" (That's what you call disingenuous.)

But Rabbit knew, and The Raven knew that Rabbit knew: he was "bird or fiend." Or both. Or worse. That poor man, asking for balm in Gilead from this creature; that's the very definition of a lost soul.

Rabbit asked, "What brings you to the forest? Shouldn't you be out shopping for Sulphur-scented potpourri, so you don't get homesick?"

"Bold words, Rabbit." The Raven glared at him, then at Elephant, which caused our gentle pachyderm to consider hightailing it the river, hopping in and floating home to his mother. "My beak can find its mark."

"With all due respect to your boss, you should shove off. The forest has little tolerance for your unpleasantness." Rabbit was this close to summoning Ronsard The Pill Bug—the one who moved Brinlaf The Whale a couple of thousand miles north-north-east with the tiniest of gestures—to send The Raven to a place called Anywhere-But-Here.

The Raven knew this was not his turf: he's a creature for the "real" world, where there is an abundance of tasty fare, and there is easy access to the all-you-can-eat buffet euphemistically called Human Frailty. He fluttered his ebony wings, glowered at his immune audience, then seemed to float upwards while, inexplicably, seeming to grow larger as he ascended, so large that his shadow briefly eclipsed the entire forest in a darkness that was darker than any shadow. It was, briefly, night.

Elephant was sweating torrents. "That bird is terrible." He shook as if he were trying to get a bug off him. It was the Shake of Yuckiness.

Rabbit was great at keeping his composure, but he was happy that The Raven was gone. "You know what's sad? That bird is one of the smartest creatures on this planet. And I'm including Beverly The Redheaded Pine Sawfly, Steve The Forest Tent Caterpillar, Denny The Sirex Woodwasp, Lamar The Badger, and Liv The Lynx."

"Smarter than Denny… and Liv?!" (Where's the interrobang when you need it?) (Where's the interrobang when you need it?) (Where the heck is the…. oh, never mind.) (Telling stories is hard.) (Actually, the stories are easy; the punctuation is hard.)

Rabbit was saying: "That bird. It's funny: he knows humans better than he knows birds; he knows humans inside and out. He gets them. He and his boss have been everywhere. Literally. No one else has. So, he's seen everything. Imagine!"

Elephant said, "You sound like you like him."

"Like? No. I like intelligence. Experience. Understanding. I admire that he has seen so much, been places we can never go. He can go anywhere….but one. His boss saw to that a long time ago. Yet he still knows more about it, that one place, than anyone else. You have to admit it's pretty impressive. Funny that the poet saw him as "a non-reasoning creature" merely "capable of speech"! Makes me think that the bird had a better understanding of the man, than the man, the bird.

"Non-reasoning"! Talk about your irony."

Elephant shook again. "He's not like a writing desk at all." He remembered that from a story.

"Of course not. How are you going to balance a writing desk on a bust of Pallas? On the other hand, a writing desk on top of the head of the goddess of Wisdom does make sense. On the other other hand, "The Writing Desk" would be a great title for a poem. I'd read that."

Elephant tried – he really tried – to process this stream of either cleverness or inanity from his friend. He couldn't. "Is it possible, "he asked, "to think too much? I mean, aren't we supposed to be, like, creatures of Nature, all natural, you know, like feelings and stuff. You know, not like arithmetic."

Rabbit replied, "Did I ever tell you about Fibonacci? Bilateral Symmetry? Pinecones? Honeycombs? Nature is Math heaven!"

You know what elephants can't do? They can't cover their ears. It's times like these that little things like this can come in handy.

# 4

# And One More: Layers

One day... well, by now you know the drill... One day, Rabbit and Elephant were staring into everywhere, when a little brown rabbit hopped over to them. This was a blue rabbit. Not the color, the mood, and if you've ever seen a melancholy rabbit, you know it is indeed a sad sight.

"I have problems," said the little rabbit.

"You've come to the right place, little rabbit," said our Rabbit. "I am renowned for my peerless wisdom from one side of this rock that I'm leaning on, clear to the other side of this very same rock. We're talking three or four feet, easily."

Elephant said, "It's true. He's been called wise-acre, wise-guy, wisenheimer, many times." He beamed with pride for his friend of no mean repute.

"Why are you sad?" asked Rabbit.

"That's one of the problems: I'm not sure. I'm not even sure my problems are inside or outside, if you know what I mean."

"Well, little rabbit, first we have to narrow it down. Yes, there are inside problems and outside problems; the latter are the easier to address; the former are much more complicated because there is exactly one outside, but there are layers and layers of inside.

"Problems that were with you when you popped into the world, problems that were created outside, then stuffed inside you without you even knowing it… It's tricky stuff."

The little rabbit followed this. "I know what you mean," he said. He looked around as if he were looking for the problems, not unlike the attempt to physically brush the chip from one's shoulder or pull the monkey off one's back or straighten one's head. They all fall into the category of "No Avail."

Elephant offered him a carrot. The little rabbit said, "Um, no thanks. I could go for a slice of pizza."

Rabbit said, "If you go across the road and follow the creek a ways, you'll see a mall. On the other side is a pizza joint. The eggplant slices are terrific. A little olive oil on top and voila!"

The little rabbit actually cheered up. "That sounds good." Rabbit gave him a few spondolas and said, "On me."

"Thanks, dad," said the little rabbit, and away he hopped, maybe a tiny bit happier, hopefully, a tiny bit happier.

"You're welcome, son," said Rabbit, but he said it so softly the odds are the little rabbit didn't hear it. We can argue later if it mattered.

Oh, the moral. The moral is, pizza is better than advice because pizza will actually be consumed and far more often it is good. Parents, take note.

# VII

*The road to When*

# 1

# The Road *of* When

### a lexington-avenue-6-subway-line diatribe by Charley Manheim

It was a late-fall evening and the sun and trees were doing their coruscating twilight thing, when Rabbit and Elephant made a sharp turn to avoid the glare. This took them to the stairs that lead to the subway platform for the downtown Lexington avenue 6 train on 68th street. Elephant was a bit nervous because he saw signs for Hunter College; the idea that such an entity existed made him shudder: a college for hunters? No, thanks. Rabbit cleared up that little false alarm so Elephant could focus on all those things that humans try so hard not to focus on: the gloom, the dankness, the dirt, the crowds, the noise, the thunderous noise, the screeching noise, the jostling, the kind of inhumanity that unwanted closeness generates, and so on.

With a roar, the train arrived. To Elephant, it was a filthy steel dragon with a hundred mouths that humans voluntarily fed themselves into, despite ending in a preposition, if it were not for that penultimate phrase that this ultimate phrase, which is actually a dependent clause, and that other dependent clause that turned the penultimate phrase into the antepenultimate phrase, and, oh, crap, it's a grammatical vortex. Quick! Get in!

It is a dreamer's dream to see an Elephant get into a crowded subway car. And Voila! The result was nothing. Zip. Zilch. No one looked up from his or her cell phone; people moved to make room without making eye contact with Elephant, though Rabbit got nudged a bit. So, if anyone asks, if you add an Elephant to a crowded subway car, the net net is it's just another delightful commute home.

One passenger - a veteran of the New York City subway system - had something to say, partly because he was intelligent; partly because he was crazy as bat stew; partly because he was a junkie; partly because he was indigent; and partly because he was out to prove that he could be just as invisible and irrelevant to his fellow riders as was Elephant. His name was Charley Manheim, a name familiar to all those subscribers to the now-defunct Luxbert, Mississippi Monthly Pendulum, "A Forum for Thought." Charley spoke, chanted, urged, expostulated, ranted —or so it seemed—to his captive and inattentive audience. One could certainly argue whether an inattentive audience is really an audience, but we can circle back to this oxymoron, later. His usual wild gesticulations - the invisible sledge-hammer move and the invisible-headlock move, for instance - had to be curtailed because there was no room to move his arms.

# 2

# Thus Spoke Charley

Patience! We invented clocks to race them,
to be chased by them!

They are monsters made by men;
they are juggernauts. Run!

The road Of When is a crowded subway car
full of Whens waiting for those doors to open

The road To When is the tracks, littered with garbage,
an homage to the city of dungeons and cells.

Sooner or later, you will reach your stop.
What's in a name? It's a stop.
But you refuse to read the semantics on the wall,
Writ large.

And the ones who stay on the train?
Look at them. The ones who have no When.
Time-forsaken. Their progress is measured by broken teeth and unfinished....
Could they be more finished? All that remains for them is
The artist's signature.
.....
Will something happen?
The door opens. Is that it?
You made the sale. Is that it?
You finished the paper. Is that it?
You stand, you sit.......

And then what?
The stairs.
putting our faces
six inches from the bloated cellulite buttocks
detailed in yoga pants that must have been tested
on Volkswagons.

We reach for what is before us
A hand, perhaps, or a handle or map
because it is before us and

perhaps it will guide us.
We hope it says something,
Moves us along the tracks To When.

The road To When takes us, moves us to
Of When. Or so we want to believe. Lurching
and jerking and jostling and balancing and leaning
and buffeting and shifting, eyes wanting to close from
too much or not enough.

Movement is sensation without substance,
the joke of volition, the absurdity of control.
Our existence wildly overstated,
an invention, a silly exaggeration

Now is a magic word,
a magic trick,
pretending to turn nothing into something.

Now is
not When, for
If it were,
It would not be!

These last lines sounded so meaningful in that Buddha-like way, but it could have been babble, too. Rabbit thought the "too" was the right word: why could it not be both? Profundity to one can be Unintelligibility to another? And who is right? The one who ascribes meaning to the meaningless? Or the one who is unable to understand what has been said, perhaps something of great value?

Charley then spoke to himself or at himself: "This is my eternal Now. I have been chewed and swallowed. I know. I know how I look. I know the weight of my existence." He is never more than half-heard, which on the 6 train, is greater than most. Is there any place on Earth where less is heard? The rumble is deliberate: its purpose is to deny words and thoughts.

Luckily, in addition to Rabbit and Elephant, a Nymph was in attendance. Here is her counterpoint:

# 3

# The Nymph's Reply

Pretending to turn nothing into something! That's the road of which we speak: converting When to Now.

How outlandish!

To think there is anything we do, *ex nihil nihilo*, my foot!

Oh, yes, we mix and mold and move and tie and twist and

we make images and sounds and

- crazier! nay, impossible! - we make images and sounds and thoughts

materialize in the mind!

It's a difficult question, this something from nothing: shall we try?

We'll keep it short

Nothing is what does not touch us.

Accusations fly: Solipsism. Blindness deliberate or not. Selfish,
self-centered, oblivious, dreamers, fools!
The temerity! The audacity!

Nothing is what does not touch us. Worse: Nothing is what we do not touch.
The world is the candle. We are the flame.
We are the reverse-creators, the un-shapers, the erasers.
The makers of puddles. With our heat and our tears,
killing grass and flowers and trees. Bladders of ammonia.

All this Now is too much for the world.
Now is a focused flame
If we moved forward faster, perhaps the world would last.
Our lingering is intolerable. Our aversion to transience…
Not here.

Do not despair!
There is a place where lingering is allowed,

Where we are invited to endure.
A place that is impervious to the flame of Now,
Immune to that futile intensity –
The feverish hunger for permanence that incinerates
Its fiery insistence for eternity.

Come! We warned you about dawdling, about delaying,
about clinging to Now.
The place is not far,
Indeed, it is far from far.
Eternal, yes, but
Eternally changing,
Moving in all directions at all times,
The leaves and breezes and streams,
The creatures visible and invisible,
The bark of the trees, hint of snakes.
Rocks, too,
Change minutely and massively
In immeasurable moments.
It is the Life of the forest,
The magical forest.

Bring only yourself,
But please leave your self behind.
One does not wear gloves to touch
Eternity.

Adieu, Subway.

# Epilogue

# Epilogue: Meaning the Beginning

Meaningful quote: (that we don't entirely understand, but it's almost too good to be true, and we say "almost" because nothing should be too good to be true. You'd think.)

> *The unmoving man at the top of the hundred-foot pole,*
> *Though he has gained entry, he is not yet real.*
> *Atop the hundred-foot pole, he should step forward - The whole universe in the ten directions is his whole body.*

(A Zen/koan/Buddha thing)

Outside, it was raining. Elephant's and Rabbit's usual booth in the diner was literally standing-room only. Skib had the map. The Map. Drawn on parchment, browning and wonderfully frail - as precious things should be - bordered with images magical to those unfamiliar with that medium, and expected by those familiar with it, were clouds that bellowed the winds; dragons and serpents; crowns of long-dead kings; rays of sunlight and starlight that did not quite reach the outlines of earthly lands; a compass without a point; words that appeared to be a cross between Coptic and Cimmerian; and a maple-syrup stain courtesy of a certain pachyderm to be left unnamed.

It was a map of everything.

Around it, besides Skib, Rabbit, Elephant, were Mr. Winter; Blinky; Sid; the Knight and his Shadow; Pearl; Hermetacles The Seal; Mel The Horse; Mike and Pete; Awesome Earl the Spider; Nextat Bat; the night manager; Marjorie the Basilisk; Hidney; Tracy and Nosmo; Lanford; the Seafarer; the Wanderer; Andromeda Rood; …seated, standing, hovering, clinging, flying, swinging, but all rapt.

On the map was a very small but unmissable X.

Elephant asked, "What is that X?"

"That X," answered Rabbit, "is Now."

"You mean Here? The Diner?"

"The Diner? No. This place hadn't been built yet when this map was drawn. This is Now."

"What about Later?"

Everyone turned to look at Elephant; they all smiled, then looked back down at the map for the answer. The cloud responsible for the Northern Winds filled his cheeks and blew a gust that moved the X off the map.

"So much for Later," said Rabbit, and everyone clapped with joy.

# Postlude

As the sun sets on another day
in the magical forest....

Do you recall the time that contained our friends reclining on the grass when they heard behind them a voice that asked, "Excuse me. Can you tell me where I can find the two who are called Elephant and Rabbit?' This was the episode that introduced us to Cass Tiron, the young woman who, back home, was known as the Socrates of Springsly, Montana, a town of 300 at its most bustling back in 1850, which was when she left the town to wander the two worlds: the noumenal and the phenomenal. She sought the whole kit and caboodle. I call it the Unattainable. Others call it If

You Can See It, It Ain't It. It has many, many other names, none helpful.

"I'm Rabbit. And this is Elephant. You've found us."

"How do I know?" She asked this question as if she had asked it many times before in an epistemological context.

"Know what?"

"How do I know that you are the two I'm looking for?"

"You make an excellent point. There could be other pairings of Elephants and Rabbits, though I don't know of any, personally. There is Belinda the Badger and Johann The Pelican. Tripley The Automechanic and Scorslin The Galaxy. Febdill The Bobcat and Delores The Retired School-bus Driver. Kinp The Sound and Cradl The Pebble. Also…"

"Got it. I have a feeling I've found the right Rabbit and Elephant. I am relieved. I am content." She sat on the ground before them and crossed her legs Buddha-like. She even closed her eyes for a few seconds and inhaled.

Elephant whispered to Rabbit, "What is she doing?"

"She's living in the moment. Taking it in. Absorbing the world, if you will."

Elephant said, "Doesn't every creature do that? I mean that Absorbing thing?"

Rabbit whispered, "No. Some creatures – I won't name names – can't or won't. Some creatures construct their own little world and even that tiny, little world that they built themselves, that they chose themselves, is too much to take in. They wish they could run away from the very world they made."

"But why would they want to create a different world in the first place?" Elephant made a circling motion with his trunk, meaning to encompass the universe, and said, "This place seems pretty nice."

"You're asking a great question, my friend, but you should probably ask Turisian The Condor that question. He's kind of the resident psychiatrist and specializes in homo sapiens sapiens."

"What's that?"

"Humans. The most recent version. Updated." Rabbit laughed at the irony.

Cass opened her eyes.

She reached into her pouch and pulled out a well-traveled apple. And by well-traveled, we mean poorly-traveled: this was one mealy, brown, shriveled piece of fruit. When Rabbit saw it, he asked Cass to give it to him. She did.

Rabbit said, "I think we can do better," and he turned to Elephant, asking him to pluck something a bit more edible for their guest. Reaching up with his trunk to what was irrefutably an oak tree, he pulled down an apple. Then a peach. A pear. An orange. A banana, which Cass had never seen before. She was amazed at this feat, which emboldened Elephant to really show his stuff: he gave the tree a nudge and all kinds of fruit fell before them. The tree – Marvis The Oak - was not thrilled: "Hey, I can do without the pushing. Help yourselves to the goods, but keep your trunk off my trunk, if you know what I mean." They all apologized. Sometimes even good intentions and fun can yield a brimming bucket of negativity.

Is this ringing bells?

Rabbit asked Cass, "Why were you looking for us?"

Cass said, "I heard that the two of you can help me."

"How? We're pretty simple fare when it comes to wisdom and all that sagacious stuff."

Cass smiled. "That's exactly what the truly wise pers… I mean, Rabbit would say. I think this is a good thing happening right now."

Elephant thought of something. He gently tapped Marvis and asked, "Do you have any fries up there? Or maybe pancakes?"

You could literally feel Marvis the oak harrumph: all of his leaves went up at the same time and back down at the same time. Then he said, "I'm not a diner." Elephant said, "Okay," and slid a few feet away from what was now a petulant Oak.

Cass said, "Show me the way."

Rabbit asked, "Don't you want to take a little break? A rest? You've been traveling for, like, a hundred and fifty years."

"More. But I found some shortcuts."

Elephant asked Rabbit, "Shortcuts? Wasn't she just outside of here the whole time?"

"Sometimes creatures can walk around and around and just not see or just keep missing this place."

Cass said something about her journey: "You would be amazed at some of the places I've been. Some have boxes, all kinds of boxes! Some that make ice! Some that can make a room cold or warm! Some that travel on wheels so you don't need a horse! Some that make music…or they call it music. Sometimes I'm not so sure."

Rabbit proffered that what Cass was seeing were not different places, but different times.

She thought that was a pretty neat idea. "But none of them had a box that gave them…"

Even Elephant knew the end of this sentence: "…Happiness."

Rabbit said, "Stay here. Stay with us."

"But what if I leave?"

Rabbit explained with a little analogy: "Sometimes, when you finish a book, you close it, turn it over and look at the cover, and you might even open it again to the first page and read that first paragraph again. To see if it means the same thing or if the meaning has changed a bit. Sometimes, you never open the book again, but it's now a part of you. It's inside you. And sometimes not. This place will always be here for you. Inside and outside. The great thing is, you get to choose."

Cass glowed. Case closed.

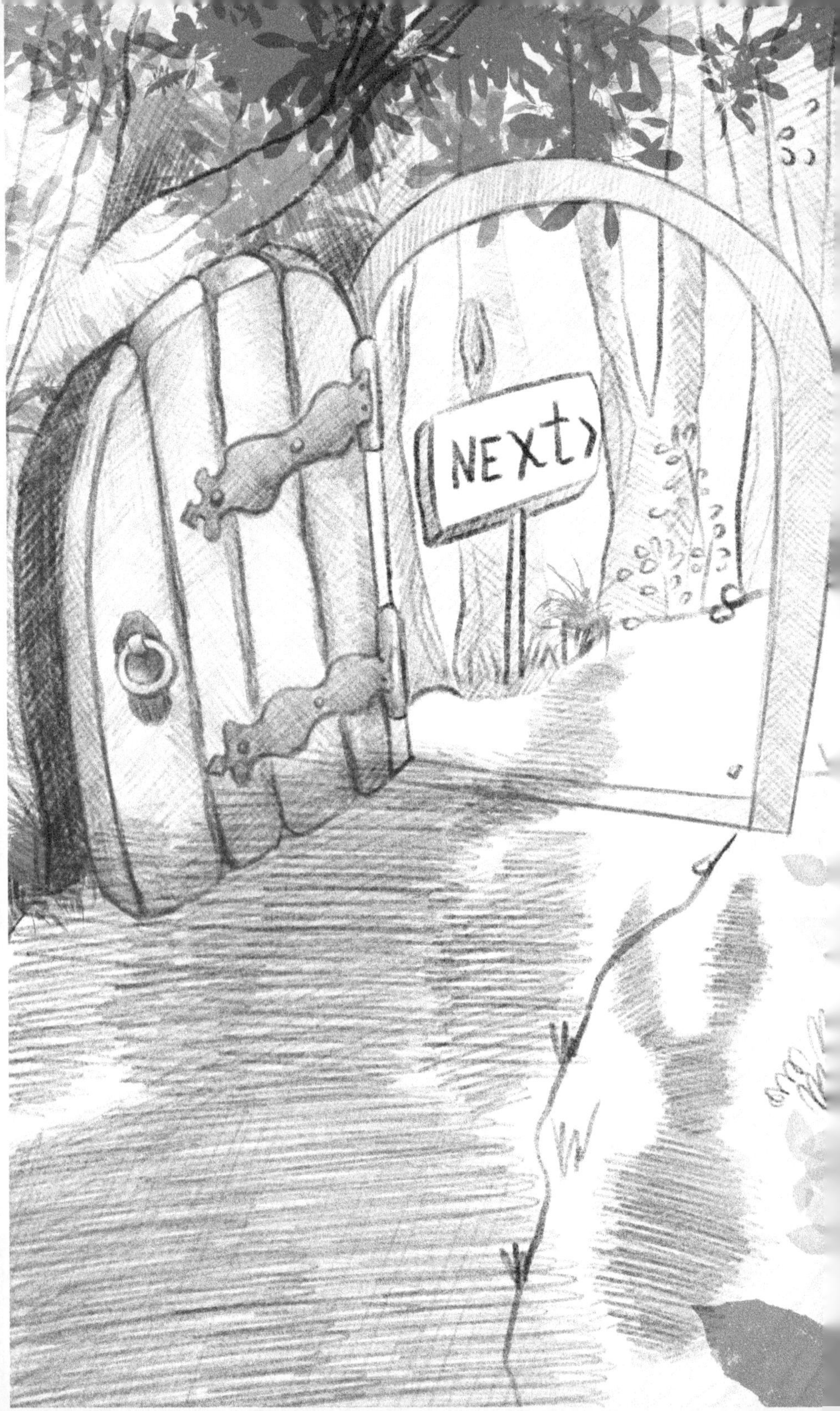
NEXT>

Our shadows grow beneath a setting sun.
(Is it possible the Timeless Day can be done?)
Nature has many paths, many doors,
Disguised as leaf-laden branches and quiet shores.
Our elongated shadows lead or follow,
Unfazed, seemingly oblivious to mountain and hollow,
Bending and contorting their shapes as the topography bids.
As the topography bids, we follow or chase, like kids.
And kids we are in the Timeless Day that still must end;
Yet, the Time abides when you are blessed with a friend.

- *T.A. Young*

Also by T.A. Young

# Elephant And Rabbit As Told By Skib Bricluster

*Where it all began: The first book in the Elephant and Rabbit series*

Savvy Rabbit and naive Elephant are the most endearing fictional duo since Tom and Huck. Philosophers without peer, they ponder everything from the existential dilemma of a particular snowflake to how to get a whale out of a river and back to the fjords (oh, wait: they really did that). They meet a drooling panther with an old grudge, a chicken with an inferiority complex, and Elephant's mother, who has come to reclaim her son. Can the friendship of Elephant and Rabbit withstand these pressures? And when they face a Tier II dragon, can Rabbit hide his eye roll?

Young's incomparable wit and depth will make you laugh out loud and leave you pondering.

"Magical, meaningful, and hilarious!"

Illustrated by Theodore Gallmeyer.

*The greatest book ever written. Period.*
— Shiva Matimbres, *The Daily Cubicle*

# ELEPHANT AND RABBIT

## AS TOLD BY SKIB BRICLUSTER

T. A. Young

Also by T.A. Young

# The Fairy Tale Book of Bifford C. Wellington

Birds become trees, and trees, birds; stars and old men change positions as easily as changing seats.

Welcome to the fantastical world of The Fairy Tale Book of Bifford C. Wellington, a collection of stories from the elusive T. A. Young. The usual hierarchy of fairy tale characters is gone – all have their say, and we relish the words equally for their wisdom and silliness. But who is Bifford C. Wellington? Who really wrote these stories? Does it matter? We find out at the end of the book…or do we?

Among the tales: an aardvark has an accidental encounter with a seamstress, Horace the Frog heads west to find his story, and a critical snail offends The Number Three. Lyrical, profound, and very funny.

Illustrated by Theodore Gallmeyer.

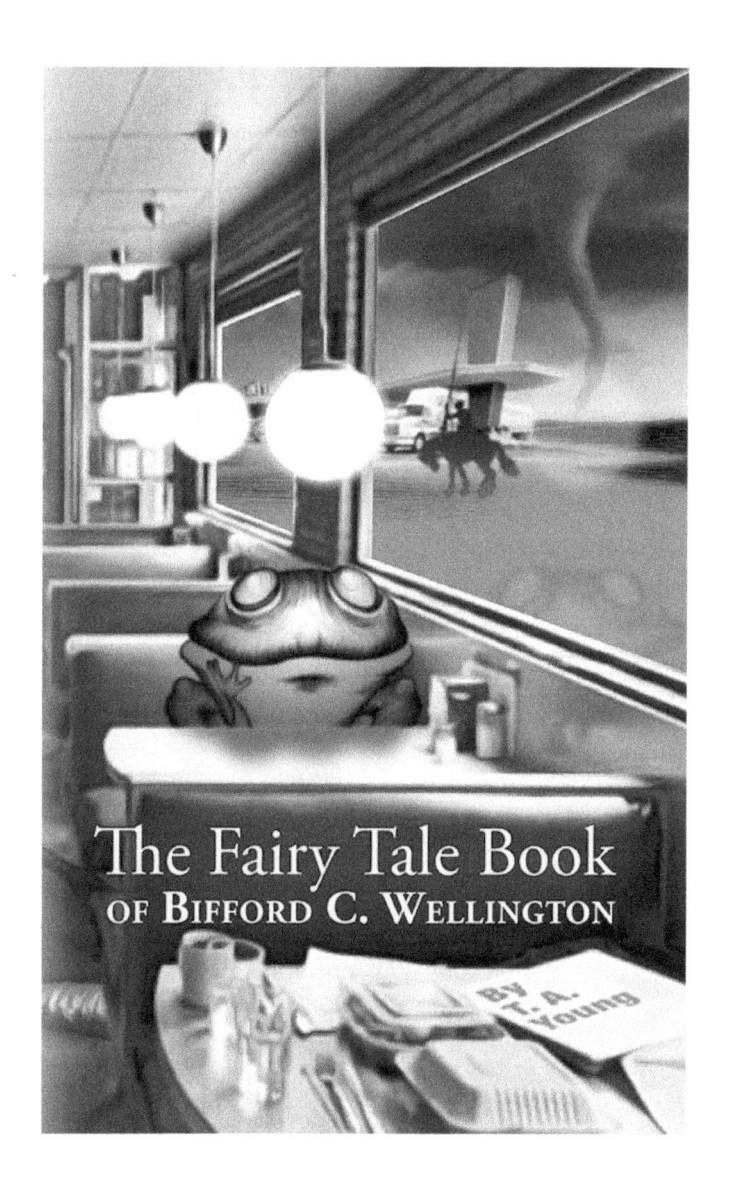

# The Fairy Tale Book
## OF BIFFORD C. WELLINGTON

BY
T. A.
Young

By Marian Grudko and T.A. Young

# Claudine: A Fairy Tale for Exceptional Grownups

*Claudine was a ladybug who wanted more than anything to live in Paris. Surely, she belonged there. Her red and black ensemble was equal to any creation from the House of Dior. And surely she would be noticed by the greatest directors of film: she bore a striking resemblance (did she not?) to the beautiful actress, Marion Cotillard...*

Claudine sets out with naive certainty to live an enchanted life, when – Of course there are surprises. And terrible challenges. Can Claudine find the strength of soul to achieve her destiny? Will she really be helped by Pierre, a sometime-rooster who quotes Simone de Beauvoir?

Marian Grudko and T.A. Young have written a book that begins as a children's story and evolves through language and thought to earn its subtitle, *A Fairy Tale for Exceptional Grownups.* With drawings of Claudine by Donal Partelow and paintings of Paris by Renée Gauvin.

# Claudine

*A Fairy Tale for Exceptional Grownups*
by Marian Grudko and T.A. Young

CPSIA information can be obtained
at www.ICGtesting.com
Printed in the USA
BVHW031845050123
655639BV00004B/129